ISBN-13: 978-0-9909293-5-2

UNFORGIVEN

BY
STEPHANIE ERICKSON

For Grandma Joyce.
Hopefully you can finish this one,
since there probably aren't any
interruptions in heaven.
We miss you.

ONE

I cursed myself every day for my innate instinct to breathe in and out. Because if I stopped, maybe the pain would stop too.

Life without my best friend Maddie was a living nightmare. My rock, my one constant, was gone. How could the sea be expected to keep the tides without the moon there to guide her? And yet, I stubbornly continued to exist, aimless and without direction.

I was not allowed to attend her funeral. David said it would be too dangerous, not only for me, but for Maddie's family. My father, it seemed, was taking his protective role seriously. So instead of saying goodbye, I spent my days in my new room with the lights off, willing the world around me to disappear.

Owen had risked making a single trip to my old apartment to get some of my things—my keyboard and my guitar, most of my clothes, the sheets off my bed, as well as a few personal belongings. Even if David had allowed me to go back, I wouldn't have had the heart to dismantle the space that Maddie had decorated.

In an attempt to cheer me up, Owen had even set up my things. When I opened my eyes long enough to see what he'd accomplished, it wasn't a bad attempt.

He'd arranged my twin bed in the corner on the far side

of the room and hung an abstract picture of a piano from my apartment behind it to serve as an artsy headboard. But my old bed had been a double, so my black-and-red comforter slumped to the ground on two sides. The TV sat across from the bed, on top of a five-drawer dresser provided by the Unseen, the mind-reading organization I'd sacrificed everything to join. The dresser offered more than enough space for all of my clothes, but I preferred a closet. It was another adjustment I couldn't wrap my head around at the moment. My guitar and keyboard were set up on the far end of the small, narrow room, and that was that. It was functional and had some elements of home, but it just wasn't how Maddie would've done it.

What's worse, I had no idea how Maddie would've organized the space. I never learned her secret—but all she'd needed was a few hours to transform any room or apartment into a homey, uncluttered, and functional haven. The sparsely decorated room felt unoccupied, despite a few touches from home. But, if I was honest with myself, I didn't really occupy the space at all. I was buried beneath a haze of grief.

In one fell swoop, I'd lost everything. The path I'd been walking on for years had been erased—both by the choices I'd consciously made and the ones that had been made for me— yet, in my grief, I couldn't see the path that now lay before me. With no direction and nothing to lead me but my sorrow, I spent my days and nights buried beneath ill-fitting covers in a strange bed, in a life I no longer recognized.

I closed my eyes, praying for sleep to claim me, but all I could see was her face. Her clear blue eyes sparkled at me as she smiled, and her red hair spilled all around her face, framing it perfectly. But then I opened them again and she was gone, making the pain worse than ever.

Owen tried to help. He brought me meals that largely went untouched and forced me to drink water. That just made me angry, because it meant I'd have to leave my sanctuary and trudge to the bathroom, where I was exposed to the real world. Life went on in that world. Things like going to the bathroom, taking showers, and eating meals went on with or without Maddie. People laughed and cried and watched TV and talked about other things. I couldn't comprehend that.

Oddly, Mitchell was one of my biggest advocates. Owen's best friend was quiet—incredibly so—but somehow, his silent companionship was more comforting than any advice and encouragement the others offered me. When he was around, I felt... understood. He didn't want me to feel anything except what I was feeling. Most of the time, he would come by with Owen, but occasionally, he'd visit alone.

Once, I heard him and Owen whispering near the door of my room.

"Just give her time," Mitchell said. "She'll come through it eventually."

"How much longer until eventually happens, Mitch?" he asked.

I didn't hear the answer. Instead, I snuggled down deeper into the covers.

David came to see me once or twice, but seeing as our relationship was relatively new, he never quite found the words to say. He would just stand near the edge of my bed, opening and closing his mouth, as if about to speak, and then change his mind. Once, while I was pretending to sleep, I saw him reach out for me, but he must have thought better of it because he turned to leave instead.

Tracy only stopped in once.

"I'm sorry for your loss. Let me know when you're ready to work." Her words were brief and stern, but oddly, full of sympathy. I wasn't ready for them, so I kept my back to her and stared at the wall, following the cracks in the paint with my eyes.

Finally, about ten days after Maddie's death, Owen reached his breaking point. "You have got to get up," he said simply.

I didn't respond. His words barely even penetrated my grief, so rather than acknowledge them, I continued to stare at the changing images on the TV.

He jerked the comforter off me and tossed it into a heap on the floor. My pajama bottoms were hiked up to my knees from all my thrashing around. The T-shirt I had on was stained and probably smelled from being worn for days on end. My brown, curly hair had turned into a ratty mass that dominated the space above my shoulders, barely leaving my face visible. I preferred it that way. Because if he could see my face, he'd know how broken I felt.

I curled into a ball and turned my back to him, shielding myself from the outside world, the one that didn't have my Maddie in it anymore. But the outside world was through with letting me ignore it.

He scooped me out of bed, ignoring my whines of protest. "Come on. I have a surprise for you. But you have to get up to get it."

After carrying me down the hall and into the bathroom, he opened one of the stall doors and unceremoniously plopped me onto one of the toilets. Thankfully, no one else seemed to be in the bathroom at the time, although I didn't pick my head up long enough to do a thorough scan. Based on the awful TV programming Owen had torn me away from, I estimated it to be midday, which would explain the absence of people. Most likely, they were all either on the work floor researching their next targets or out on assignments, tracking down potential threats to society with their abilities. Silently, I thanked him for choosing this time to drag me back into the world of the living. That way, no one else had to see what I'd become, at least not yet.

He knelt down in front of me and placed his hands on my knees. I didn't look at him, hiding instead behind my mop of hair. He reached up and tried to tuck some of it behind my ear, but he only managed to get his hand tangled in the mess. After a few minutes of struggling, tugging, and painful pulling, he was free.

"Well, now that I've thoroughly ruined the moment, please get yourself showered. I'm going to wait here for you. You can talk to me if you want… or not. Just know that I am here."

I didn't nod or acknowledge that he'd spoken in any way. I just stared down at the floor of the bathroom. There were precisely fourteen small, yellow tiles in my view. I counted them again.

"I can stand here all day, Mac. David's given me some time off, in light of your... condition," Owen said as he leaned against the wall opposite me.

Finally, I tore my eyes away from the fourteen tiles at my feet and looked up at him. It was the first time I'd done so in days. How was it that he hadn't changed at all? My world had collapsed in on me, and yet, he knelt in front of me, perfectly put together in a clean T-shirt and cargo shorts. His black waves had recently been combed, and despite everything I'd become, his gorgeous, dark eyes did not look away from me. There was no judgment or expectation in his expression, only hope, and maybe a little sadness. It made my chin quiver.

He sighed. "Mac, I'm sorry." It wasn't much, but it was enough. He held his arms out to me, and I climbed into them. His clean scent enveloped me, bringing the comfort only he could give. Although I'd cried in his arms a lot over the last several days, this time felt different, like it was washing away some of the haze that cocooned me. Not all of it, but some.

I wasn't sure how long he let me cry, but eventually, I took a breath and sat back to look at him. I didn't speak. I couldn't. Not yet.

He gazed deep into my swollen eyes. "You're welcome." He paused, and then wiped one side of my soaked face. "Now, quit your blubbering and take a shower. You're a snotty mess."

The old me would've laughed and swatted at him. But that girl was gone. There was no trace of her anywhere. And this new girl I'd become didn't know who she was... or how to laugh. So I just stared blankly at him.

He chuckled awkwardly. "All right, Mac. Go get in the shower. I'll be right here when you're done."

At his prompting, my body stood, as if by its own will, and went into the nearest stall. They were all divided into two sections. An outer curtain concealed a small space equipped with a bench for your clothing, and then the actual shower stall was behind a glass door. I was grateful these showers had doors. Shower curtains were useless—if there was any kind of gentle breeze, they ended up getting stuck to your wet skin.

The water came on hot, and steam soon engulfed the stall and fogged up the door. I stood watching it for a moment, numb to everything.

Slowly and methodically, I peeled my days' old clothing away from my skin, threw them on the bench, and stepped into the steaming water, shutting the door behind me. At first, I just stood there, letting the water fall on me, willing it to wash the memories away. When it didn't, I sighed and actually started washing. Each stall was equipped with men and women's toiletries, organized in small cabinets built into the wall of the stall. They were well stocked and typically had a variety of shampoos, conditioners, shower gels, and soaps.

My hair was very nearly a lost cause, and I seriously considered shaving my head for a moment. I searched the cabinet for a comb, but I came up empty. After using about half a bottle of conditioner, I gave up and decided to get out.

With one towel wrapped around my rat's nest and a second around my body, I exited the stall. True to his word, Owen was waiting for me where I'd left him. "Ah. Good. You're still alive. You just about steamed me out."

I stood looking at him, waiting for my next directive. "I didn't bring you any clothes, so you'll have to get dressed in your room." He held out his arm, pointing in the direction he wanted me to go, and I silently went. After stopping to scoop up my dirty clothes from the bathroom floor, he followed close behind me.

Once in my room, I picked out a T-shirt and a pair of knit shorts while he waited outside for me. I didn't bother to make sure my outfit matched. In fact, I couldn't stop looking at my bed. The comforter was still on the floor where Owen had left it, but I could easily remedy that. It looked so inviting, in a rumpled sort of way.

Before my train of thought could get much farther out of the station, Owen knocked. When I didn't respond, he came in. "Hey, don't go getting any ideas," he said, clearly noticing the way I was lusting after my bed.

He pulled my rolling stool out from under my keyboard and

sat me on it, sitting across from me on the bed. "Thought the bed might be too tempting for you."

Of course, he was right.

"So, listen. I told you I have a surprise for you, and I do. This thing called Coda is coming to town."

That caught my attention. Coda had been a big deal in my former community. Orchestras from all over the world came together to perform in a three-day music festival. As much as I'd always wanted to go, it had never been a realistic consideration. For one thing, it was always held in another state or even another country. For another, I never had the money for traveling, let alone for tickets to the event. One year, I had actually summoned the courage to ask the woman I'd believed to be my aunt to lend me the money. Needless to say, I didn't end up going that year either.

So it had seemed like a once-in-a-lifetime opportunity when I found out it would be held in town this year. I had even called Maddie about it, and we daydreamed about going together.

But my bestie wasn't around to go with me anymore. It hadn't occurred to me that Owen might want to go in her stead.

Owen smiled at my obvious interest in his topic of choice, pulling a folded brochure out of his back pocket. It was wrinkled from the steam in the bathroom, but still legible. It boasted the London Symphony Orchestra, the Chicago Symphony Orchestra, and the LA Philharmonic. But their featured orchestra was the Royal Concertgebouw—the best one in the world. I gasped when I saw their name. They had never performed in Florida before.

The old me tugged at the pieces of my heart desperately, not wanting to miss this opportunity. I traced the bold, yellow letters of THE ROYAL CONCERTGEBOUW with my finger.

"I thought you might like to go," Owen said quietly, resting his hand on my knee.

I looked up at him, torn between knowing he was right and wrong. He'd been watching me, searching for some sign of life.

Gazing into his beautiful, brown eyes so full of hope, it was hard to deny him. But could I really go without Maddie, knowing it was something we'd intended to experience together?

Trying to rescue me from my floundering, Owen spoke up again. "I thought I might like to go with you. Maybe brush up on my Gasbag de la noot?" It was a special joke between us—his purposeful mispronunciation of the piece I dreamed of mastering on the piano. He paused for a moment. "Especially since I haven't heard you play it for a while."

His observation made me flinch. I hadn't played since the day after Maddie's death, the day I agreed to be part of the Unseen. I'd seen her spirit so plainly, leaning against the piano so she could listen to me play, her face drawn into a relaxed smile. I could almost hear her humming along, her beautiful voice a soft whisper carried along by the notes I banged out of the piano. Part of me wanted desperately to play again, just to bring her back. Another part of me was terrified she wouldn't be there this time. Maybe she'd said her goodbyes that night, and I'd never see her again. If I didn't play at all, I could still hold onto those slender threads of hope.

"So, what do you say?"

I looked down at the pamphlet again. The festival was being held at my alma mater, Florida State. The performances would be in several auditoriums, so people could easily walk from one concert to the next. It was a great venue for the prestigious event, and it would only cement the school's reputation as the premier music school in the area. Over twenty thousand people were expected to attend, *so book your seats today*, the brochure implored.

As much as I wanted to stay locked up in my room—in my grief—forever, I knew I couldn't. I tried to smile at him, but it was like my face had forgotten how. So I nodded instead.

His face lit up as he jumped up from the bed and scooped me into his arms. Hugging me close, he spun around, and I caught the stool with my legs. It rolled across the room, but Owen didn't even notice. He was too joyful.

He kissed me earnestly, which surprised me. We hadn't shared a real kiss in quite some time. Sensing my need for space, he'd kissed away my tears, kissed my forehead when we parted ways, things like that, but this was different. It was full of potential—potential for our future, for the life we could share if I wanted it.

He smiled from ear to ear as he set me down. "This will be so fun, and hopefully, it's just what you need to remind you of who you are."

That was an awfully lofty expectation for Coda, despite the fact I had long considered it a once-in-a-lifetime opportunity, but I didn't want to kill his enthusiasm.

For the first time since the day Maddie died, I found my voice. It was raspy and cracked with disuse, but it was there, waiting for me. "Thank you," I said and weakly attempted to clear my throat.

Owen beamed at me. "Wow. You could totally play a Star Wars villain with that voice."

Again, I felt like I should smile, and I almost wanted to. Almost.

Thinking of everything he'd done for me—and how little I'd given back—I blurted out, "Owen, why are you being so good to me?" The question had plagued me for days.

He sighed. "I know what you're going through, Mac, and I don't expect anything from you, if that's what you think. I'm here to let you know you're not alone. I'm not going to lie—I hope we can have a more two-sided relationship when you're ready—but we don't have to decide that now. Until then, all I want to do is be there for you."

It was the perfect answer, and it reminded me of exactly why Owen had captured my heart, why I'd wanted to be with him once all the secrets between us fell away. Could he fill the void Maddie had left in my life? No, probably not. But could his love heal my broken heart? Maybe, if I was willing to let it.

I tried to smile at him, but the effort was too much. I'd already said thank you, so I was left with nothing, no way to show him my gratitude.

He smiled knowingly and saved me from saying more. "Maybe you'd like to join me for a movie? Remember, I have the whole day off to celebrate that you're rejoining the world." He held his hand out for me to take, looking at me with that same hope in his eye. This time, my chin didn't quiver. My tears were spent, for now.

But my exhaustion wasn't. I glanced back at my bed. This was the most action I'd had in days. It was enough for me, but apparently not for Owen.

"Come on. It'll be fun," he promised, still holding his hand out for me.

Silently, I took his hand and followed him upstairs. Just like that, I rejoined the world of the living, but the ghosts of my past followed close behind.

TWO

The days that followed my shower were a blur of being paraded around the facility and kept busy playing video games, doing mindless chores, or watching movies. Owen suggested playing the piano a few times, but I evaded him.

Aside from Owen, I continued to spend a lot of time with Mitchell. It was too much effort to try and form new friendships with any of the girls in the Unseen. They weren't unkind to me, but I kept them at a distance, and they all seemed fine with that.

Mitchell and I often sat in silence in the main room, no pressure on either of us to speak. He might sit on one couch with his legs stretched out in front of him, reading a book or listening to some podcast he'd found, while I would lay on the adjoining couch, staring off into my haze, our bodies following the L-shape of the furniture. We hardly ever turned on the TV, despite its huge, imposing presence on the other side of the room. Mitchell never asked me if I wanted something to read—he just let me sit—and because of that, I found him very comforting. He was there if I wanted to talk, but he never seemed disappointed if I didn't.

David kept his distance for the most part, and I appreciated his decision to give me some space. I couldn't deal with the constant drain of my grief, let alone form a relationship with my long-lost father.

But, eventually, he called me into his office, apparently tired of waiting for me to seek him out. "Hi," he said after I sat down in front of his desk, the simple greeting delivered almost cautiously.

I looked at him, not feeling like that needed a response. Responses required too much effort, for very little return. At any rate, everyone seemed to be getting used to my new, quieter nature, so he didn't miss a beat when I didn't answer him.

"It's been over two weeks since…" He paused. "Since you moved in with us. I think it's time for you to return to your training. Tracy is ready to begin tomorrow."

"Okay."

"Are you ready?"

I shrugged.

David sighed. "Now look, I know you feel like you've lost everything, but I wish you could see that you've gained a few things too. You're not alone here, Mackenzie. We're all trying to give you some space, but I have to tell you, your attitude is less than encouraging. You have the most potential of anyone I've ever seen come through my office. Will you throw that away because you're too blinded by your grief to seize the life that's in front of you?"

My eyes narrowed as anger loosened my tongue. He wasn't my father any more than the woman I'd grown up with was my aunt. "So, now you want to give me some fatherly advice?"

The beginnings of a frown formed on his face. "No, I'm just trying to help."

"You want to help?" My anger was flowing freely now that the dam had broken. "How about throwing some understanding my way, instead of judging me for the poor way I'm handling my grief?"

His frown gained traction, and I frowned back. We sat there that way for a few minutes, our disapproval for each other mirrored on our faces. Finally, I asked, "Anything else?"

"No," he said, clearly unhappy with me.

I got up and left, considering David's reaction to me. The

old Mac would've been upset that I'd stepped out of line and would've wanted to correct it. But the new girl couldn't find the will to care. It was easier to just let everyone's concern flow off me.

Owen met me in the gym outside David's office, like always. "How'd it go?"

"How is it that no matter where you are with a job, you're always here waiting for me whenever I'm done with training or a meeting?" It came out sharper than I'd intended—almost like an accusation. I reminded myself that my irritation was with David, not with Owen. The hurt look on his face made me regret speaking at all.

"I'm sorry, I didn't mean it like that," I amended. "Thank you for being here."

He nodded. "I just happen to be good at managing my duties. That, and I asked to be given only research jobs for the next few weeks while you—" he paused, seeming to search for the words, "—while you ease back into things."

I smiled and took his hand as we walked toward the stairwell.

"So, how did it go?" he asked again.

"They want me to start training again." I decided not to say anything about David's little pep talk. Talking about it would mean going places I wasn't in the mood to go, giving explanations I wasn't ready to give, feeling things I didn't want to feel. Better to pretend it hadn't happened.

"That's good news, right?" He looked at me, searching my face for some kind of indication of how I felt, but it was an ill-fated mission. I felt nothing—well, nothing but grief.

"When do you start?"

"Tomorrow, I guess."

We walked upstairs together. When he squeezed my hand, I wasn't sure which one of us he was trying to reassure.

That night, Mitchell and I sat alone in the gym while Owen did some research for a confidential job. He didn't tell me the details, and I didn't ask—not because I was afraid he wouldn't tell me, but because my heart wasn't in it, at least not yet. The main room was full of nightly movie watchers, and I was still avoiding the library where my piano was kept, so we retreated downstairs.

He was lifting some free weights in front of the wall of mirrors while I sat on the floor, pulling at a thread in one of the mats.

"I'm going to start training again tomorrow."

"Mmm," he said as he curled the twenty-pounder to his chest.

"I don't want to."

"I know."

Instead of getting upset at his simplistic response and lack of encouragement, I only felt relief. He *did* know how I felt, but he didn't judge me, try to tell me I should be ready, or encourage me to refuse.

In that moment, it was enough. At least, it was enough to get me through to the next day.

In the morning, I met Tracy promptly at eight in my designated training room. I hadn't seen the tiny space for a few weeks, and when I walked in, it made me long for the days before I'd been consumed by grief, the days when I had simply been eager to learn. I wondered how well the new me would do with training. The old Mac had excelled, but the person in the training room at that moment couldn't summon the will to care. My attitude should have disgusted me, but it didn't.

Tracy didn't acknowledge my struggle or any of the things that had happened to me in the previous weeks, which I appreciated. Everyone else looked at me like they didn't know what to say. Tracy knew exactly what to say, and it was all business.

"Today, we begin working on entering other people's minds. Now, I know you've already done that, with a ranger or something?"

"A trail guide, yeah." I thought back to that day at the park with Owen. It seemed like it was years, not weeks, ago. Searching the guide's mind for information about the caverns we were exploring had been so easy—natural, almost. Now it felt like something someone else had done.

"Fine, you obviously know how to reach out. That's great. You're ahead of the ball game. But, it's a whole different sport to do it with someone who has defenses like yours in place."

I hadn't really thought about it. In fact, I'd never considered forcibly entering someone's mind. All the minds I'd ever read had just been there for the reading. But going into someone's head when he or she didn't want you there? "So, how *do* you get past someone's defenses?"

"Creatively." I didn't think she was going to elaborate, but for once, she threw me a bone. "It's best to craft your tactic based on how the person has constructed his or her defenses. Some people, like Owen, just go charging in."

I chuckled without smiling, remembering how he'd come barreling into my mind on the stairs the day I'd told him I could push people out. His approach was less than elegant to say the least.

"Indeed. You'll find that his approach doesn't work for everyone. Subtlety can take longer, but it can prove to be a valuable skill if you are able to master it."

"Subtlety…" I said, trailing off. How did you go about subtly entering someone's mind? Particularly someone who didn't want you there?

"I can talk to you about it until I'm blue in the face, but like everything else, you need to experiment with it for yourself." Her blonde hair bounced as she shrugged her shoulders. "What works for me might not work for you, Owen, or David. Everyone's different. If you learn nothing else, remember that adaptation is vital."

I nodded and took a deep breath, trying to clear my head. But Maddie remained. She smiled at me from the corner of my mind. Really, I didn't even want to push her all the way out. What if I couldn't get her back? Deciding to proceed with my mental companion, I closed my eyes.

"Whenever you're ready," Tracy said.

Reaching out, I found her easily. I couldn't tell if she'd done that on purpose, or if it just came naturally to me. But I could still feel her in the room when I closed my eyes. It wasn't like I could hear her breathing or moving around; I could feel her mind working, and I moved toward the feeling.

"Good," she said. "What do you see?"

Looking around, I found myself in a battlefield. Smoke or fog rose around me, but through the haze, I could make out a barbed-wire fence that seemed to stretch on indefinitely in both directions. The grass leading up to the barbed wire looked like it had been trampled and worn down nearly to the dirt below. Where there wasn't grass, pits of dirt appeared, as if mines had gone off at some point. I wondered if they really had, or if Tracy had arranged it this way purposefully to sow the seed of fear into intruders. Either way, it was effective.

In spite of myself, I watched my step as I got closer, and spotted some trenches beyond the fence. But the most impressive and intimidating defense was a huge wall that climbed as high as I could see, disappearing into the haze.

"It's a war zone."

"Just the way I like it." I could hear the smile in Tracy's voice. "So, what's your move?"

"I'm not sure, to be honest." Maddie silently walked beside me along the edge of the barbed wire. A breeze I didn't feel seemed to be constantly blowing her hair away from her face and ruffling her flowered skirt. Wishing she would comment or offer some advice, I searched in vain for a break or a weak spot in the fence.

"Tracy, is everyone's mind like this? Does my mind look like this?" I wasn't sure what I wanted her to say as I explored the chaotic landscape. Had there really been a battle there? Had lives been lost? I shivered at the thought as I walked on.

"No, not everyone's mind is like this. I don't really know what yours is like, in light of recent events."

Opening my eyes, I tore myself away from her mind and landed back in the training room. "What do you mean? Someone's visual mind can change based on their mental state?"

"Absolutely. Grief can be a weakness, giving easy access to intruders. Or it can be a trap, sucking you into a black hole of depression. As I expect yours is the latter, I have no intention of finding out for sure."

"What makes you say that?" I asked, curious to know why she thought I wasn't weak in my grief. I certainly felt weak. Heck, I was barely functional.

She frowned at me. "Depression is a dangerous game. One I'm not prepared to discuss with you at the moment. Today, your task is getting into my mind. Let's focus on that."

"But maybe if I understood, I could get over it faster." It just came out. I didn't mean it. Or maybe I did, who knew? The one thing I did know was that I wanted to know what it was about my grief that made my mind so dangerous.

She hesitated, and I could tell I'd hooked her a little. In the end, she shook her head. "Not today, Mackenzie. We need to stay focused on the task at hand."

Reluctantly, I nodded and closed my eyes again. I found myself back on the battlefield without difficulty, but no matter how far I walked, I couldn't find a weakness in her barbed wire. I looked beyond it, knowing this was just her outer defense. The challenges ahead would be even more difficult to overcome.

Eventually, I worked up the courage to try and jump over it. I laid a hand on the wire, trying to get some leverage, and was zapped by some kind of current.

"Ouch," I said as my eyes flew open. I examined my hand for signs of visible damage. Finding none, I turned my hand over in front of her, as if to prove that the shock had hurt badly despite the fact that it had left no mark.

"Reality is a fluid concept in the world of the mind. It's real because your mind believes it to be. You feel pain because your mind tells your hand it has been shocked. Just because there's no physical evidence of the event doesn't make it any less real."

I thought about that concept for a moment, deciding it made sense to me. No one could see my pain over Maddie, but that didn't make it any less real for me.

We worked for hours, but I made no further progress, and my hand still smarted at the end of day.

Tracy sighed and stretched. "Let's break for today. I think

we've both had enough. We'll revisit this tomorrow." She stood abruptly and left me alone in the training room. There was no encouragement, no 'good job today' or 'good effort.' But then, Tracy wasn't big on unnecessary praise.

David was apparently waiting for her outside. The door was open just enough that I could hear their muted conversation.

"How did it go?" he asked.

"She lacks the focus and drive she once had," Tracy said in a low voice. "I don't know how to help her. I didn't react this way to my own losses. I felt them, sure, but the drive to honor the people I'd lost was stronger than the pull of grief." She paused for a moment, and I considered her words. Was I really dishonoring Maddie with my actions? "I'm worried about her, David."

"You're not alone on that front," he said and they both walked away, leaving me alone in my haze.

A few moments later, Owen knocked lightly on the open door. "Hey. How'd it go?"

I didn't answer him. I just stared at the wall, feeling like I'd failed Maddie all over again. But how could I summon the strength to honor her? I could barely get myself out of bed every day.

"That well, huh?" He pulled Tracy's chair up next to me and glanced at the spot on the wall I was currently boring my eyes into.

I opened my mouth to tell him what Tracy had said, to pour my heart out to him. Maybe I would feel better for it. Maybe he would tell me she was wrong, that I wasn't dishonoring Maddie. But the haze weighed down my tongue. Closing my mouth again, I wondered what good it would do to tell him. What did it even matter?

"It doesn't matter." I pasted on a fake smile that probably looked more like a grimace and patted his knee. Then I stood to leave the room.

"Hey, wait up," he called after me. "Aren't you coming to dinner?"

"Sure," I said, stopping in my tracks for just long enough for him to reach me. Thinking about Tracy's battlefield, I wondered again what my own mind would look like to an intruder. *Haze, nothing but an oppressive, suffocating haze.* A dark smile crept across my lips as I thought about one of the Potestas getting hopelessly lost in my haze. *Maybe then those murderous bastards would get their due for killing Maddie.*

Owen eyed me. "What?"

"Nothing." I needed to redirect him, but that required effort, speaking. But the worry that he would continue to question me about my training, and that I might end up telling him what Tracy had said afterwards, loosened my tongue. "Hey, have you ever gotten into Tracy's mind?" I rarely asked him questions or initiated conversation anymore, so he jumped at the chance to engage with me.

Owen took my hand in his as we climbed the steps, making our way toward the dining room. "Heck no. I don't know if anyone has. I take it you saw her defenses?"

"Yeah. I'm a little creeped out by her war zone."

He chuckled. "Yeah, Tracy's a unique woman."

Hearing people's thoughts for years and years was completely different from deliberately entering someone's mind. I had no idea what most minds looked like on the inside, despite my years of listening. "So, what is a normal woman's mind like?"

His laughter echoed off the walls of the stairwell. "There is no normal when it comes to women. Most men are pretty simplistic. They tend to compartmentalize, and most of them never have more than one compartment open at any given moment."

"I don't really know what that means."

Shaking his head, he said, "No, but you will. Once you get the hang of things, you'll blow past Tracy's defenses, and everyone else's for that matter. I'm sure of it."

"Did you?"

"I got past the barbed wire, but not the trenches. She let me advance once I was past that."

So, there could be advancement without perfection. But to achieve the bare minimum, I had to get past the fence. "How'd you manage that?"

"I just took a running leap. Maybe not the most elegant approach." He shrugged. "Scratched me to ribbons and shocked the heck out of me, but it worked."

I felt a frown crease my forehead. I wasn't sure I had the strength to jump over the fence, particularly after my attempt that afternoon. It was at least two feet wide, and as tall as I was. I thought of Maddie's silent, almost companionable, presence with me in Tracy's mind. Maybe she could help me vault over. It wasn't the subtle solution Tracy wanted, but it might work.

The question of whether Owen had ever brought his lost loved ones with him into someone else's mind hovered on my lips. But I shook my head. No, he would most likely tell me that I needed to focus, that mind reading was dangerous if you weren't one hundred percent in the moment. It was best to keep my silent companion to myself.

As we ate dinner in silence, I vowed to at least try to jump Tracy's fence the next day. After all, what did I have to lose?

The following day, Maddie and I found ourselves facing the barbed wire again. I turned to her. "Wanna give me a lift?"

She didn't react, only stared straight ahead. I'd never tried to engage her before, and I regretted it almost immediately. In life, she'd always been so full of energy, but the form next to me was stony and lifeless. The smile on her face looked like it had been pasted there. My Maddie would've offered suggestions as we went along, chattering nonstop about how we could break down Tracy's defenses. She never would've kept a silent vigil by my side. She would've dived right into the problem, getting it wrong right along with me until we got it right.

I tapped her arm a few times, trying to get her attention, but her skin wasn't soft and warm like it should have been. It was hard, unyielding, and cold. "Could you help me out?" I said quietly, becoming more and more unsure of my decision to keep her with me.

Again, she didn't respond. I stared into her face. It held the same smiling expression, but a sinking certainty slowly settled in. It wasn't her. My Maddie would've walked through fire for me.

My Maddie *did* walk through fire for me. This wasn't my Maddie. It was a ghost, a poor excuse for her memory. Nothing more; nothing less.

I collapsed onto the cold, damp ground of Tracy's mind.

As soon as I hit the gravel, Maddie turned to ash and blew away on a gentle breeze, leaving me utterly alone on the battlefield.

"Who are you talking to?" Tracy asked.

A sob at the back of my throat held the answer behind it.

Seeing my pained expression, she released me for the day, and I didn't hesitate to leave. Practically running from the room, I pushed past Owen and ran straight to my room where my bed awaited me.

THREE

In the days that followed, I didn't have any luck getting past Tracy's defenses. Owen tried to comfort me, but his concern was plain in the way he tiptoed around me. He tried to be encouraging at every opportunity, and never pushed me to do anything I wasn't ready for, but I could see the worry in his eyes. Tracy seemed more and more concerned with each passing day.

But I just couldn't bring myself to try very hard. As soon as I found myself in her mental landscape, I would just sit Indian style in front of the barbed wire fence day after day, unable to properly concentrate on the task at hand. All I could think about was the image of Maddie disintegrating in front of me and how alone I felt on, and off, that battlefield.

She's left me forever, I thought one afternoon as the dew from Tracy's battlefield seeped through my yoga pants. But the cold couldn't compete with the shivers of loneliness wracking my body at that moment.

After a week had passed with no progress, Tracy took action.

I sat across from her and started to enter her mind, but she stopped me. "Today, we're just going to talk."

"What?" Tracy never wanted to talk. My curiosity threatened to part the haze.

"It has never taken you this long to make progress with your training. You might not master a skill right away, but you can at least stumble toward achieving it." She paused, searching my face. "I can tell you're not even trying."

What was I supposed to say to that? She was right, I wasn't trying, and I didn't want to try. I just wanted to be left alone.

You are alone. The thought nearly loosed the sob I was keeping at bay in the back of my throat.

She sighed. "You know, Mackenzie, I understand how you feel. I've lost friends, family, loved ones." She paused. "Seems like everyone I get close to is eventually taken from me."

My grief turned to anger in a flash, and I glared at her. If she'd felt losses too, why couldn't she throw me a rope? Because she'd honored her loved ones by working harder, not despairing? She thought my depression was a weakness. "Turns out I'm not so special after all, huh?" I sneered. "Everyone's got some sob story here. You all know what I'm going through, but somehow, no one can understand my behavior." I stood up, but before I stormed out, I threw one last barb Tracy's way.

"I guess I've dishonored Maddie for too long, hmm? I must be a lost cause."

I started toward the door, but I didn't make it two steps before Tracy's vice-like grip snatched my arm. "What do you mean, you've dishonored Maddie?"

"I heard what you said to David about how you reacted differently to your losses. And how my actions are dishonoring Maddie's memory." I looked at her accusingly, practically spitting the words at her.

She let go of my arm. "That's not exactly what I said. And just because we handle our grief differently doesn't mean I'm right and you're wrong. It just means I'm not sure how best to help you."

I sank back down into my chair, pouting, although I wasn't really sure why. Tracy wasn't wrong in her assessment. Then again, neither was I.

We sat in stalemate for a few moments until Tracy softly spoke up. "Mackenzie, think about how hurt you are over Maddie's death. Don't you want to work hard to keep it from happening again, if not for you, then for someone else? Think of another young woman losing her best friend. Why would you wish that on someone?"

"I don't," I said after a few heartbreaking beats.

"But your actions, or lack thereof, say you do."

I thought about that for a moment. I had been taking Owen and the Unseen for granted. What if they needed me to be an active part of their team? What if my lack of care helped lead to their downfall? Then I would really be alone. The thought made me shudder.

Tracy leaned forward, her blue eyes boring into what was left of my hazy soul. "You have the power to defeat the Potestas once and for all. After everything they've done to you, why wouldn't you want to seize that power?"

My eyes narrowed as I thought of all the ways I would harm them if I ever found out who they were. They would beg for death before I was done with them; I would make sure of that. "I do," I said, my voice low and menacing.

Tracy sat back in her chair, a satisfied smile on her face. "Then let's get to work."

The rest of the training day was frustrating for me. My new resolve made me daring. I finally tried vaulting over her barbed wire, but I didn't get enough speed or height and ended up in a tangled mess. The barbed wire poked into my arms and legs, and the fence gave me the shock of a lifetime. Tracy laughed at me as I tried to soothe my invisible wounds on the other side of the training room.

"Decided not to go with a subtle approach, eh?" she said through her laughter.

My glare just made her laugh harder.

"I suppose that's enough for today." She looked at me as she stood. "It was a good effort today, if unsuccessful. That's all I want from you. Effort."

I nodded, still rubbing my arms as she walked out.

That night, as Owen and I ate dinner in the dining room, I couldn't concentrate on the conversation unfurling around us. At least it wasn't because of my haze this time. It was because of Tracy's barbed wire. How could I get past it?

"So, are you getting excited about Coda?" Owen asked me.

"What?" I looked up at him, trying to replay what he'd said. "Oh, yeah. Sure."

He frowned. "Sure seems like it." He stabbed at his food, clearly frustrated with me.

In that moment, I felt bad about my behavior. He'd done something thoughtful and kind to try to make me feel better, and I'd basically ignored it. "You're right. I'm sorry." I reached across the table and touched his hand to let him know I meant it. He looked up from his plate, a hopeful expression on his face. "I'm trying," I said simply.

He turned his hand over and grabbed mine. "I know."

Our hands remained entwined as we ate in silence for a few moments, until I couldn't stand it anymore. "I tried jumping the fence today."

"Oh? How'd it go?"

I cringed at the memory. My arms still ached, and I felt a little twitchy from the shock.

"That good, huh? So, what's your next move?"

"I honestly don't know. I'm out of ideas."

"Wow, you're in trouble if your only idea was one of mine."

I balled up my napkin and threw it at him, and he laughed louder than the situation warranted.

Mitchell sat a few seats down from us, trying to give us some space to eat together. But I wanted to pick his brain. "Hey Mitchell," I called out. He looked up and nodded. "How did you get past Tracy's defenses?"

"Well, I—" Just as I was about to get my answer, I spotted Tracy carrying her dinner plate across the room. She walked over and put a hand on Mitchell's shoulder.

"He got creative. Perhaps that's something you should consider, instead of stealing ideas from your colleagues. Out in the field, you'll have no one but yourself to rely on," she said. After giving me a disapproving frown that made me feel about five years old, she walked away.

"Great," I said. "I've disappointed her again." It was out of my mouth before I could stop it, and I cringed, bracing myself for Owen's reaction.

But he didn't bombard me with questions or encouragement. He simply moved the conversation to lighter things. "I was thinking I'd rent a limo for Coda. Really show my girl a good time."

"That sounds great." I said, successfully forcing a small smile. The emotion wasn't there, but at least I knew my face could still form the expression.

"Maybe you should get a new dress to wear. You know, just for fun."

"Maybe I should." But the thought of shopping without Maddie threatened to throw me back into darkness. "Maybe I can borrow something from one of the other girls." Seeing the disappointment crowd in on his expression, I added, "The festival is three days long. Who can afford three brand-new fancy dresses anyway?"

"Being awfully presumptuous, aren't we? I never said I'd take you to all three days." He smiled mischievously behind his fork as he stabbed at his salad.

"Oh, well, I'm not planning to miss any of the days. I can always find another date if you're not willing. I hear I'm quite exceptional." I didn't really feel that special after my morning with Tracy, but I said it anyway. Perhaps faking confidence would help me feel it once more.

"Yes, well, being exceptional is an attractive quality." The desire in his eyes was hard to ignore.

It sparked something deep inside me, something that had been lying dormant for weeks. But before it could catch, I went back to eating my dinner, feeling drained from the effort of holding back the haze. Mitchell eyed me from across the table, and he gave me a knowing nod.

Honestly, I would've welcomed some quiet time with Mitchell, but Owen was done with his research for the moment, so that meant a movie after dinner. I dreaded the nightly movie, since my bed was calling to me more loudly than ever. But at least it would relieve me of social obligations such as talking. If Owen had wanted to go for a walk, play a game with the others, or do anything else requiring some kind of interaction from me, I might have collapsed right there in front of him.

No, that night, I didn't need to exchange pleasantries. I needed .. what? Peace. To figure out how to get into Tracy's mind. Maddie's face floated across my mind's eye once more—that same lifeless Maddie who'd accompanied me to the war zone. A sob bubbled at the back of my throat, but it didn't make it nearly as close to escaping, which I considered a win.

After the movie, I went to bed with visions of Tracy, her battlefield, Maddie, and my old life swirling in my head, unable to find peace as they all warred for space and the haze threatened at the edges of my mind.

The following day, I sat in front of Tracy's fence, wondering what to do. Then a sudden thought occurred to me. Something Tracy had said about reality. What was it?

Reality is a fluid concept in the world of the mind. It's real because your mind believes it to be.

I looked at her fence, knowing it wasn't real. None of it was. The reality was that I was sitting in the training room in a particularly uncomfortable metal chair across from a hard-as-nails woman who was both trying to keep me out of her mind and secretly hoping I'd get in. I wasn't on an old battlefield. It wasn't a relic of death and destruction from long ago. It was Tracy's made-up ruse to keep people at a distance, and it worked.

"It's not real," I said aloud as I stretched out my hand toward the fence. Closing my hand over one of the barbs, I didn't brace myself for the stabbing to come or the shock of electricity. It wasn't real, and I finally knew it. The barb passed through my hand as if I were a ghost.

I waited silently for Tracy's response, thinking she'd notice I discovered her weakness. Surprisingly, she said nothing, so I stood up and took a step toward her fence. One more and I'd be right in the middle of it, or it would be right in the middle of me. It was an odd feeling to have a barbed wire fence go straight through the center of your body. My body screamed that there should be some kind of sensation, but I forced my mind to remain calm.

It's not real, I repeated to myself. Slowly, in no more than four steps, I walked straight through the fence that had kept me at bay for weeks. When I reached the other side, I turned to look back to look at the battlefield I'd finally crossed. I wanted to dance, to celebrate my victory, but I didn't. Tracy hadn't seemed to notice my breach, and I didn't want to draw attention to myself yet. I wanted to see just how far I could go. I pushed on.

Approaching the trenches slowly, I peered down into them. Owen had said he never made it past the trenches, but he hadn't told me why. It made me leery. A yellow fog hung inside, obstructing the view to the bottom. *Mustard gas?* I wondered.

Squatting down at the edge of the trench, I debated what to do. It was too wide to just jump over. I'd have to climb through it, which meant breathing in whatever that yellow fog was. It would get on my skin, in my eyes, and in my lungs. I imagined it burning holes in my clothes, leaving me coughing and clawing at my eyes. Just the thought was enough to make me want to turn around. *It's either real or it isn't,* I told myself as I hopped down into the abyss.

The instinct to cough was overwhelming. To squelch it, I took a deep breath and swallowed, reminding myself that the gas was a creation of Tracy's mind. When I took in a deep breath, it was the air in the training room that was entering my lungs, not the yellow fog that surrounded my subconscious self.

Turned out the trench wasn't that deep, just tall enough to cover my head. If I stood on my tiptoes, I could barely see over the edge of it. I walked to the other side, working hard to not get disoriented, and hoisted myself back onto the battlefield.

Looking back toward the fence, I silently congratulated myself, feeling like my accomplishment warranted some kind of fanfare. *Two down. One to go.*

But when I turned around again, I realized an immense and

foreboding wall of dark bricks stood in front of me. Stretching as far and as high as I could see, it loomed over me. Smooth to the touch, there was no way to climb it, and I feared I could walk forever and never come to the end of it. There was no gate, no weak point, no corners, not even a tiny little storm drain. This wall had been built to keep people out, and it served its purpose well.

Thinking my approach for the last two barriers would work just as well on this one, I told myself it wasn't real and walked confidently toward it. I crashed face-first into the bricks. My immediate instinct was to soothe my hurt, but I didn't want to open my eyes and alert Tracy to the fact I'd made it this far. It was time to finish what I'd started. So I got up, brushed off my shorts, and tried to come up with a different approach.

As I narrowed my gaze, I realized I could see images within the bricks. I brought my face so close that my injured nose touched Tracy's wall. It was cool against my skin, and my breath left a fog on its dark surface. As I narrowed my focus on one of the bricks, the scene expanded before my eyes. I could see a book in Tracy's lap. The image became increasingly clear the longer I watched it, and soon, I could even read the words in the book. It was about strategy, specifically war strategy. I pulled back and it dawned on me that they weren't just images and scenes, they were *memories*.

I examined another brick. Tracy was in a meeting with David.

"I'm looking at a new candidate," he said, pushing a folder across his desk toward her. Suddenly, I was a fly on the wall in a very real way. It was odd and exhilarating at the same time.

She opened the file, and I saw my picture clipped to the left side.

"What makes her so special?" she asked, thumbing through the papers inside the file.

She's too old, with no previous training. This one's going to be a nightmare. Her thoughts sounded a lot like her voice, only they had a faint echo.

Fearing I'd be thrown from her mind if I didn't concentrate,

I ignored the sting of her early impression of me.

"Mitchell pointed her out. I was going to leave her alone, but he said her skill is making her feel isolated."

Tracy closed my file and set it back down on David's desk. "Isolation isn't always such a bad thing. And I've never known you to take someone on out of pity. She doesn't seem to be in danger, and based on what Mitchell has seen of her abilities, they're not anything too extraordinary. So, what's really going on here?"

David pulled my file closer to him and opened it, gazing at my photo with a hint of affection in his eyes. "Her true identity is classified for now." He looked up at Tracy. "But know that she is special, and if she does decide to join us, I'm confident she would be a great asset."

I've never seen David like this before. He's almost sentimental. I wonder who the girl is. Tracy's voice echoed again through my mind.

I continued to walk along the wall, stopping to watch a memory every now and then. The farther I went, the older the memories were. The wall went on forever in both directions, and I found myself wondering what the other direction held. If the blocks were made of memories, why didn't it end at present day? But I was too enthralled with watching Tracy train with the Unseen to go back to check.

Then I saw something I would never be able to forget. It was a memory from her life before the Unseen. Tracy was a teenager, walking next to a girl who was her spitting image.

I didn't know Tracy was a twin, I thought.

The two girls were so alike. They even had the same swagger about their walk. But Tracy was clearly identifiable by the style of her dress. Her cargo shorts and loose-fitting T-shirt posed a marked contrast to her sister's feminine knee-length skirt and lacy top.

I couldn't tell where exactly they were, but people bustled around them as they walked down the nameless city's sidewalk. It seemed like a sunny, warm day, and from the look of the books in their arms and the packs on their backs, I guessed they were walking home from school.

This is going to be so fun. The voice was more chipper than Tracy's, so I figured it had to be her sister's thoughts I was hearing. But the girl in the cargo shorts was the one with a smile on her face. Confused as to which one was which, I listened eagerly.

Mom hates it when we do this. We're liable to get extra chores for a week, you know. That one sounded a lot more like Tracy, just younger and a bit higher pitched.

Worth it, her twin answered as she shrugged her shoulders. *Plus, it's a double win for me because I get to see you looking pretty.*

Tracy rolled her eyes as she adjusted the backpack she was carrying. *Yeah, well, don't get used to it.*

I started piecing it together. They had traded outfits with each other before leaving school in a ruse to confuse their mom. I had a hard time imagining Tracy pulling a prank like this, but the thought of her doing something so lighthearted made me smile.

Bumping Tracy with her hip, her sister smiled and threw an arm around her twin as they walked along the sidewalk together, effortlessly maneuvering through the crowd. Thinking there was nothing more to this memory, I was about to move on to another brick when I noticed a figure following the girls. Tracy's twin seemed to notice him too.

The man was dressed casually, in khaki pants and a polo shirt. He looked like he was on an errand for work. In fact, the only thing that made him stand out from the crowd surrounding him was the way his steel-gray eyes had zeroed in on the girls. Everyone else went about their business, not paying much attention to their surroundings. But he watched the twins hungrily, like they were his prey.

Subtly, the girls picked up their pace. Just as Tracy's twin looked over her shoulder, the man raised a pistol equipped with a silencer.

Where on Earth had that come from? How come no one noticed him carrying it? I wondered, horrified at the events unfolding in front of me. Fear crept down my spine and through all my limbs.

The moments that followed passed by in agonizingly slow motion.

Just before the man pulled the trigger, Tracy's twin darted behind her sister and grabbed her backpack, pulling her down in an effort to save them both. But it didn't work. She took the full force of the bullet.

The memory returned to normal speed as Tracy whipped around and the shooter melted into the gathering crowd.

"Call 911!" someone shouted.

Tracy cradled her sister. *Patti, stay with me. It's going to be okay. Help is coming.* Her tone was urgent, filled with fear.

But Patti didn't answer her. She smiled at Tracy one last time, and then took her last breath in her twin's arms, never saying or thinking another word.

The sorrow that filled my mind in that moment overwhelmed me completely. It felt like half my soul had been torn from my body. The pain I felt was altogether different from my grief over Maddie. It left me feeling raw, exposed, and so very vulnerable.

My eyes flew open, returning me to the real world and the training room with Tracy. I realized my face was wet with tears.

Tracy gave me a confused look. "What happened?"

I opened my mouth, but I couldn't verbalize. I felt the weight of her sister in my own arms as her soul left her body an empty shell in my lap.

"Tracy, I..."

"What?" She narrowed her eyes at me, becoming suspicious.

Clearing my throat, I tried desperately to find the words to communicate what I felt. "I'm sorry." I paused, wanting and not wanting to go on. "About your sister."

Her eyes grew wide with shock. "What the hell did you do?" She flew up out of her seat. "That was private!" she yelled, and I shrank back in my chair, with nothing to protect me from her wrath.

"I'm sorry, I just—"

"You just what? Nosed around where you didn't belong? How did you even find that?"

"I was just trying to get past your defenses, like I was told, but it—"

She cut me off again, clearly not ready or willing to hear me out. "It doesn't matter. We're done here," she said, storming out of the room, leaving me utterly alone with a sorrow more acute than anything I'd never known.

FOUR

The next morning, I was summoned bright and early to David's office, not that I'd been sleeping. The encounter with Tracy had cursed me with an unsettled, sleepless night.

Tracy was seated in one of the two chairs across from David's desk when I arrived. She didn't greet me or even make eye contact. Pleasantries were never her strong suit, but her behavior was notably cold.

Before David could talk, I tried to smooth things over with Tracy. I was afraid I'd ruined everything by trying to prove that I was good enough to hack into her mind. But now that I'd done it, and the consequences were laid bare, who had I been trying to prove myself to? "Tracy, I—"

David cut me off. "Mackenzie, please sit down. Tracy has explained some of what happened in yesterday's training. However, I'm not sure I fully understand. I'm hoping you can enlighten me."

I sat down slowly in the chair, trying to read the temperature of the room. David seemed curious, but Tracy... well, I hoped I was misreading the hostility I felt emanating from her like heat off pavement.

"I'm sorry, Tracy. Truly," I started. "I just wanted to prove to you... and me, I guess... that I could do it."

"Do what, exactly?" David asked.

"Get past her defenses. All of them."

Tracy's eyes widened. "All of them? That's how you knew about my sister?"

"Well, yeah. How else would I have known?"

She shrugged and shook her head. "David is the only one who knows what happened to Patti. He picked me up soon after that."

I nodded. "Yes, I know." I clapped my hand over my mouth as soon as it was out. For someone who hadn't been doing much talking lately, I was sure making a habit of saying too much.

"You… of course you do." She shook her head. "Is there anything you left private?"

"I stopped at your sister. I thought it was just a fun memory, and I was about to move on when I saw the guy with the gun. The rest played out in slow motion. I couldn't stop it." Just talking about it brought the images back to the forefront of my mind, making me shiver.

"I'm well aware of how the rest of it plays out, thank you." Despite her smart words, her tone was quiet and sad.

David intervened on my behalf. "Tracy, it's pretty clear she didn't do it on purpose. And I trust you'll keep what you've learned to yourself?" I nodded. "Now, it's time to tell us how you accomplished it."

"It really wasn't that hard, once I figured it out."

Tracy leaned back in her chair and folded her arms over her chest. "No one else thought it was that easy."

"It was actually something *you* said to me, Tracy, about reality." She looked sidelong at me, and I could tell she wasn't sure she wanted to hear that she was to blame for the intrusion into her memories. "I realized the things in your mind weren't real, at least not in the same sense that the things in the training room were real. They were real in our minds, which is how I got hurt by your damned barbed wire fence so many times, but it was still just a trick of the mind, right?" They both eyed me skeptically. "Once I convinced my own mind it wasn't real, I literally walked through your first two defenses."

"Even the mustard gas trench?"

"Well, yeah. The air I was breathing in the training room was fine. I just had to remind myself of that." I shrugged. "But when I tried it on your wall, I ran smack into it. Actually hurt my nose a little." I rubbed it, remembering the injury. "I had to work hard to keep my concentration, since you didn't seem to realize how far I'd gotten. Honestly, I just wanted to see how much further I could go. That's all. I wasn't trying to pry into your past or hurt you in any way. I wish I'd stopped at the wall," I said, thinking of her sister. Because of what I'd done, her sister's death had haunted me the whole night. I wanted desperately to erase what I'd seen in her mind, and I hoped she realized I hadn't snooped on her maliciously.

"Me too," she said, all the hostility draining from her, leaving her slouched and weighed down with sadness.

"So, what happened at the wall?" David asked.

"After I crashed into it, I looked at it more closely and saw that there were little scenes playing in the bricks, almost like little movies. I realized they were Tracy's memories, so I started watching them. Each time I watched one, I moved a little further down the wall. And I just kept making my way through them until I got upset by the memory of her sister."

"I see. You make it sound so easy," David said as he toyed with his mustache, seeming to consider my explanation.

We were all silent for a moment. I didn't know what to say to that. It *was* easy, once I understood the mechanics of it.

"I do have a question," I said, turning to face Tracy. "Your wall seemed to go on forever in both directions, but the memories started pretty close to the present. Why didn't it end at to-day's memories?"

"Memories, as you grow closer to present day, grow more detailed and mundane. What you wore yesterday, whether or not you flossed your teeth, what you had for lunch. The memories are smaller, but there are a lot more of them. Although not truly infinite, they're close—you're always creating new memories with each passing moment, so you're continuously adding new bricks," Tracy explained, her tone even and unreadable. I'd hoped for some sign that we were okay, that she had forgiven me, but I didn't get it.

We fell into silence again, and I held my breath as I waited for one of them to speak, not knowing if I'd violated some sacred Unseen rule. Would I face some unknown punishment for learning one of Tracy's deepest, darkest secrets? Before the panic could settle in too deeply, David spoke again.

"No one has ever made it to Tracy's wall. I've seen it, but only because she's allowed me to see it. She has put trainees, not to mention Potestas trying to hack her mind, in the hospital with her mustard gas trench." He paused, seeming to consider his next words. "No one has ever described a strategy for entering minds in such simple terms. It's revolutionary. Not to mention the skill it takes to discipline your mind that way. It's not easy to convince yourself that what you're seeing and feeling isn't real… even for those who know better." He leaned forward on his desk and looked at me so intently it unnerved me a little. "Do you understand what that means?"

I shook my head. "No."

"You could be the key to bringing the Potestas down for good."

I chewed on that statement for a while. What exactly did it mean? Maybe I could be responsible for bringing some kind of peace to our country by stopping the terrorist attacks from the Potestas once and for all. And I could bring justice to those who were responsible for Maddie's death. The thought spread its tentacles through my mind, taking root quickly. Vengeance was almost as hot a fire as hope, and once the spark was lit, the fire could become an instant blaze.

"Honestly," David said, "I don't know whether to be proud of your accomplishment or disturbed by it."

I cringed a little as I glanced at Tracy. "Yes, I'm in the same place as David," she admitted. "But mostly, I'm glad you discovered it before the Potestas did. It questions everything I've ever learned about creating defenses. I mean, if nothing I can create within my mind is real, what's to stop any old average Joe from waltzing in and stealing classified information?"

She tilted her head, as though a thought had just occurred to her. "If the first two defenses were so easy for you to walk through, why did my wall stop you?"

"I've been thinking about that a lot. The only thing I can come up with is because it's real. The memories are real... or at least your version of them is real to you."

"What does that mean?" she asked, more curious than defensive.

"Well, as I was watching the attack on your sister, I noticed you never once looked in the direction of the shooter. Yet, he appeared in the memory, plain as day. I even saw your sister notice him. None of those details were blurry or obscured as they might be in a less pivotal memory. I can only assume you read reports of the event later. Eye-witness accounts and things like that filled in the gaps, so you now have a complete picture of what happened, even if that's not how *you* saw things that day."

Her mouth hung open for a moment as she looked at me. I glanced at David, hoping for some reassurance, a tension breaker, something. He just smiled at me, his expression full of... pride?

"You know, for a music major, you have a fantastic understanding of how the mind works," David said. Tracy just sat there, stupefied.

"Well, I was a music therapy major."

He smiled again. "Yes, and on that note, I think Tracy is going to take a break from training you."

"What? Why?" I couldn't keep the alarm from my voice. "Is it normal to take a break? Am I being punished?"

David laughed. "You are absolutely not being punished. What would give you that idea?"

"Well, I violated Tracy's mind. That has to be against some sacred Unseen rule." I glanced at her, trying to gauge her reaction.

He chuckled and held up his hands. "Tracy just needs time to absorb what you've taught us, so we know what to teach you next. That's all."

I sat back, trying to understand what he was saying. They weren't punishing me, just putting me on the bench until they could figure out how to keep up with me.

"So... what should I do in the meantime?" I asked carefully, still worried I might be transferred away from what few connections I had formed.

David pushed a file across his desk to me. "You're going to start working."

FIVE

I walked out of David's office in a bit of a daze. Owen wasn't waiting for me in the gym, so after taking a quick glance at the file in my arms, I wandered up to the work floor in search of him. Unassigned workrooms were spread out along both sides of the hallway, each of them equipped with big, glass windows facing inward, which made it easy to find someone or to locate an empty room. There were at least five offices on each side of the hall, and at the end there was a bizarre little room equipped with a cot, a sink, and a toilet. I couldn't imagine that anyone would stay in there on purpose when our dorms were only a few flights of stairs away, so I could only assume it was for prisoners.

About three rooms down, I found Owen staring intently at the set of screens in front of him. I knocked lightly on the glass window. He smiled when he spotted me and immediately left his workspace to join me in the hall.

"What are you doing up here, beautiful?"

"I'm taking a break from training, apparently." I pointed to the file under my arm. "I'm going to start working."

"What?" He seemed incredulous, but I wasn't quite sure why. Did he think I couldn't handle a job? Or that I wasn't ready? That I wasn't good enough? Or that I'd be in danger? The questions cycled through my mind on rapid fire until he interrupted them.

Opening the door to his work area, he gestured for me to follow him inside. "Why don't you start at the beginning?"

Suddenly, I saw the situation from his perspective. No wonder he was startled—the last he knew, I was still having trouble launching myself over Tracy's wall. I hadn't felt much inclined to talk lately, so he knew only the bare minimum about my training. I didn't know what to say, or how to say it. Unfortunately, I couldn't tell him much more than that. I had secrets to keep, promises to uphold. Shuddering at the thought of Tracy's wall of memories, I shook my head and struggled to find a safe place to begin.

"Well, I um…" I hesitated. "To be honest, I'm not really sure how much I can tell you."

He frowned, so I decided to throw him some crumbs. "I got past Tracy's defenses. It's why they gave me my first assignment." Deliberately leaving out exactly how many of Tracy's defenses, I set the folder on the table in front of me and took a seat across from Owen. I hoped he would pick it up, thumb through it, and show some curiosity about my first assignment.

Instead, he simply glanced down at the folder with a disapproving look on his face, making my defensive side flare to life.

"What? You don't think I can do it?" Folding my arms over my chest and narrowing my eyes, I challenged him to cross me.

He looked up at me, startled by my reaction. "What? No! That's not what I was thinking at all. I'm just worried it might be too soon." He paused. "For work."

"Well, don't you worry. It's just some spying gig on a real low-profile guy. As far as I can see, his only crime is being a scientist in a suspicious field. It's essentially busywork."

He leaned back in his chair, glancing warily at the file on the table. "Nothing the Unseen does can be classified as busywork, Mac."

Although his sentiment tugged at my curiosity, I was still skeptical. I pulled the file closer and opened it to see the photo of the scientist paper-clipped to the top. I'd only thumbed through it quickly, but I'd seen enough to know he studied the

toxic effects of chemicals on humans. He was mostly responsible for doing the due diligence for those warning labels you
saw on stuff like bleach and brake fluid. Although some of his
experiments were conducted on animals, which was a bit dis-
agreeable to say the least, I wasn't sure how else someone could
discover the effects of inhaling too much ammonia mixed with
bleach. Scientist I was not.

"Well, he seems pretty harmless to me," I said, staring down
at the scientist's photo. Dr. Jeppe had brown hair, cut in an
eighties-style bowl with silver-rimmed rectangular glasses cover-
ing his brown eyes. He'd worn a white lab coat for the photo,
which looked like it had been taken for an ID badge, but that
was all I could glean from the photo. Taken from the waist up, it
was hard to tell how tall he was, but he seemed slender.

"Sooo..." He drew out the word. "Do you feel like you're
ready?"

I closed the file. "I'm not really sure what there is to be
ready for, Owen. I don't even have to leave for this 'job.'" I put
air quotes around the word with my fingers.

He lowered his voice. "I think you're taking it too lightly, but
that's just me. All of this has hit you very hard. I just don't want
you to rush into anything. There are others who can do the work
until you're ready."

I thought again of what had become of Maddie and Tracy's
twin and sighed. "Maybe. But the scientist will be a good distraction. Besides, no one else wants to take on my busywork."

He ignored my last comment and glanced at the big, black
computer screens behind him. I wasn't sure if they'd fallen
asleep while we were in the hall, or if he'd turned them off in
anticipation of me coming into his space.

"Either way," he said before I could debate it much longer.
"You'd probably better get to work. Do you know what they're
looking for, or how much time you have?"

"No."

He chuckled. "I love those kinds of assignments." I didn't
miss the sarcasm in his voice. "Just do me a favor and try to
take the scientist seriously. I can assure you he's not busywork.

And whatever intelligence you do uncover on him will be used later in an actual mission. Something you discover could save an Unseen's life."

From my cursory glance, my target just didn't strike me as the type of chemist who was secretly gassing people with his creations in some creepy dugout in the woods. I felt certain that he wasn't a threat. "Like what? What could I possibly dig up on this guy that would be that life changing?"

"I don't know." He sighed, clearly searching his mind for a good example. "Oh, I know. What if he has a nervous tic? He scratches his eyebrow when he's nervous or something like that. You put that tiny detail in your report, and if the person assigned to him sees him doing it, he or she might know the guy's onto them."

"That's a bit of a stretch. Anyway, how am I supposed to find out he has a nervous tic without meeting him? I'm not even being asked to go out into the field for this one."

"That's just an example. Everything you find out about the guy will be important. Sometimes, you never know how the details are going to add up until it's too late. Hindsight is a terribly clear picture."

His eyes pleaded with me, and the depth of his concern gave me pause. A tiny voice at the back of my mind said, *Maybe the scientist is dangerous.* But I dismissed it. As far as I could tell, sending someone after him would be a waste of our resources, so anything I put in my report wouldn't ever be implemented in a real mission anyway.

"Hey," Owen called out to me before I walked out of his workroom. "Good luck! And congrats on your first assignment."

His tone seemed sincere enough, so I nodded. "Thanks." It hadn't occurred to me to be excited about my first assignment. It meant I was a contributing member of the Unseen. But I didn't feel like it, since they obviously didn't want to trust me with anything important. I wanted to be hunting the real bad guys—killers and terrorists, particularly those who were responsible for Maddie's death—not chasing after some poor scientist who was probably just guilty of being in the wrong place at the wrong time.

As I walked down the hallway, looking for an unoccupied space, I chewed on everything that had happened recently. I found an office a few doors down from Owen's, and shut myself inside it before setting the file on the desk in front of the computer screens. Owen seemed adamant that the assignment wasn't busywork, but of course he would say that. He cared for me, so the last thing he wanted was for me to feel bad.

I should've asked him what his first assignment was, I thought. Maybe they gave unimportant assignments to all the newbies.

The room I settled into was identical to the one I'd just left. Two computer screens and a large, flat-screen television lined one wall, hallway-facing windows lined another, and the other two were covered in dry-erase boards. A long table sat in the center, with chairs on either side so you could spread out as needed. All in all, it wasn't a bad workspace, if you had to be several floors underground.

Settling in front of the screens, I typed in the scientist's name to a Google search, just to see what it would spit out at me. It popped out several scholarly papers on the science behind separating chemicals, as well as his credentials at the University of Michigan. Not much else.

As I flipped through his file again, reading the contents more intently, nothing in particular jumped out at me. I thought about going back to David's office and asking him why they were looking into this guy, maybe get some sort of jumping-off point. But then I remembered this assignment probably wasn't about the guy. It was about keeping me busy until Tracy figured out what to do with me.

A heavy sigh escaped my lips as I sat back in the desk chair and put my hands behind my head. It was going to be a long week.

By Friday, I hadn't come up with anything more. Having little else to go on, I'd printed out his papers, and I was trying valiantly to read through them. But I was a musician, not a chemist. The language was all jargon, and I found myself having to look up every other word. It was at once frustrating and tedious.

Most of his papers talked about identifying and separating the specific toxic elements of things like ammonia, trichloro (chloromethyl) silane—which I had to look up. Apparently, its toxicity was pretty intense and it was used to bond silicon and chlorine, or something like that—and a few other compounds that I didn't learn much about beyond the fact that they were highly toxic if inhaled, and some were extremely flammable.

Then something occurred to me. I pulled up Google again, typing in, "What would happen if you combined ammonia, trichloro (chloromethyl) silane, sulfur pentaflouride, and osmium tetroxide?"

Nothing popped up, except articles defining what the chemicals were and how they were all ridiculously deadly.

Leaning back in my chair, I considered the scientist's seeming fascination with identifying and isolating the most toxic elements of each of these chemicals. Assuming this was a real job, and not just busywork, what could he do if he managed to successfully combine some of the worst elements from each of these deadly chemicals? Could he create a stable super chemical that would be so horrifyingly deadly, I wouldn't even expose my worst enemies to it?

I paused for a moment, considering those who were responsible for killing Maddie. *Nothing could be bad enough for them.*

A few minutes later, I had his Facebook page pulled up on one of the screens. His last post—a humblebrag about beating the latest Final Fantasy game—was over a month old. The rest of the posts followed a similar theme: a review of the latest Marvel movie or Game of Thrones episode, a few quick words about a comic book he'd read or a game he was playing. He didn't post frequently, and he never talked about work. His most recent post about the game hadn't gleaned any comments or likes, and he didn't have many friends. But was unpopularity enough of a reason to accuse him of terrorism? Staring at his profile pic, I couldn't repress the thought that he looked like a sitcom nerd. All he needed was tape on the bridge of his glasses and a pocket protector.

No, I thought as I slammed his file shut. He was harmless.

As I added the papers I'd printed to the file, I hoped this would be the last I saw of Dr. Jeppe.

The following morning, I had a meeting with David to report my findings.

"So, what did you learn about Dr. Jeppe?"

Refraining from the urge to roll my eyes proved quite difficult. "That he's fascinated with highly toxic chemicals."

"And?"

"Not much else to be honest. He has several papers published about separating the particularly toxic elements out of certain chemicals like ammonia." I picked that one because I wasn't quite sure how to pronounce the others.

"Isolating only the toxins?" He seemed to think about that for a moment. "And how does that strike you?"

"To be honest, I don't know. I'm not a chemist, David. I don't even know what's possible. I guess there's a possibility he might be trying to learn how to combine the toxins into a super chemical or something, but I don't even know if that's possible for one thing."

"Is there another thing?"

"Well, I don't really think he's that dangerous. Just because he's chosen a somewhat dangerous career, why should that make him an automatic target? From the looks of his Facebook page, he's too interested in playing video games in his spare time to be plotting a major terrorist attack."

"Are you so confident you can judge someone's character from Facebook?" Although his question seemed accusatory, his tone was genuine, like he really wanted to know how I'd come to my conclusions based on the information available to me.

"No. I suppose not. But he doesn't exactly have many of the common characteristics of a criminal. Wouldn't it be a better gamble to use our resources elsewhere? On more of a surefire danger?"

"The atypical ones can be the most deadly. Not because they're more manipulative or sadistic, but because they're unexpected."

His comment gave me pause, and we sat in silence for a few moments.

David sat back in his chair, his eyes looking at me without seeing me. His hands tented around his full mustache. "Yes, well, thank you for your work," he said absently.

"I'm not sure how much help it was," I said, somewhat startled by his abrupt dismissal. Atypical or not, I was still convinced the scientist wasn't much of a threat.

My comment snapped David back to our conversation. "I won't know for sure until I've read your report, but I'm sure I'll find it very useful. Thank you, Mackenzie." He leaned on his desk, all business now. "You're to return to your training with Tracy this afternoon."

"I am?" A mix of excitement and nerves washed over me.

David smiled as I squirmed in my chair. "You are. Don't be late."

I stood up immediately, not wanting to give him time to change his mind. "I won't. Thank you." I rushed from his office, only to realize it was only eight thirty in the morning. My afternoon training session with Tracy was still hours away, and I knew Owen and Mitchell were both busy working on their own jobs. I paused at the library, but my demons were already sitting on the piano bench. There wasn't any room for me, so I moved on.

For the first time in a while, I didn't really want to be alone, but the only company I had was my haze. I ended up in my room listening to a Royal Concertgebouw recording of one of Mozart's concertos, letting the strings sing away the seconds until I had to meet Tracy again.

SIX

Tracy was sitting in her usual chair when I entered the training room. Her outfit of cargo shorts and a dark green T-shirt was completely wrinkle free, and I found myself wondering if she ironed her cottons. It didn't seem outside of the realm of possibility.

"Please," she said, gesturing toward my chair. Her tone was upbeat and friendly, and it unsettled me. Where was the stern, let's-get-to-work Tracy I'd come to know?

Eyeing her nervously, I took my seat and fidgeted with the drawstrings on my hooded sweatshirt.

"First of all, I'd like to apologize for my behavior."

My eyes shot off the floor and straight to her face. "What?"

She didn't repeat herself. "I was unprofessional. Moving forward, I will strive to not allow it to happen again." She eyed me. "Despite the surprises you are sure to throw my way."

I nodded, not sure what to think. To my mind, her behavior had hardly been unprofessional. I was the one who'd overstepped my bounds by invading her memories. Clearly, the mistake was mine.

"I'm sorry I overstepped." I hesitated. "And I'm sorry about your sister." The words came out almost in spite of myself—I needed to say them.

Tracy cleared her throat. "Yes, well. What's done is done." I wasn't sure if she was referring to my invasion of her mind or her sister's death, and she didn't give me a chance to sort it out before she started talking again. "I'd like to talk about why you didn't make it all the way into my mind."

"How would I even know if I did make it all the way into your mind? I was seeing your memories, your thoughts during those memories. What more is there to see and do in someone's mind?"

"Lots of things. Hear someone's live thoughts, for one thing. Controlling them for another. But those are lessons for another day. Today, I want you to tell me what went wrong."

I hadn't really considered that something had 'gone wrong' as Tracy put it. To me, I made it past all of her defenses. That had been my only goal, and I hadn't given any consideration to what might be past that. But when I thought back to the moment I was torn from Tracy's mind, I knew immediately why my time inside her mind had ended with that memory.

"I was upset." That about summed it up.

"Upset?" She frowned at me, as if she were unfamiliar with the emotion.

"By your sister's death."

"I see." She hesitated before moving on, as if searching for just the right way to help me. "Mackenzie, the people we hunt will have far more disturbing things locked away in the corners of their minds. You must guard your heart against whatever you may see, or you will be found. If you are found inside the enemy's mind, you could be lost to us forever. Worse, the things they would do to you would make whatever you had seen seem like child's play." Concern etched lines around her eyes. "I fear this may be your fatal flaw. Sympathy."

I snorted. "It could've been empathy if they hadn't hurt Maddie."

Her eyes narrowed. "Be careful of your grief. I think you'll find vengeance a terribly unsatisfying path to follow."

"How do you know? You never pursued your sister's killer." I clapped my hand over my mouth. My tone was judgmental and almost accusatory. "I'm sorry. I don't know where that came from."

"Yes. And that's why I advised you to be careful of your grief. It can turn on you in a flash."

Leaning forward, she rested her elbows on her knees. "Today, I want you to try again. I want you to show me that you can maintain your control and successfully worm all the way into my mind. But..." Her eyes turned deadly. "If you so much as breathe a word about anything you find there, I will personally flay you."

Swallowing hard, I nodded. "I wasn't aware you knew how to do that."

"I would learn," she said, her voice low and menacing. In response to my nod, she said, "Let's get to work."

"Tracy, I..." I hesitated, uncomfortable with the arrangement. "Couldn't we do this exercise with someone else? That way you could guide me along. And your secrets wouldn't keep me awake at night." Hopefully, I could choose someone whose secrets weren't as heavy as Tracy's, though I knew too well that everyone had some kind of darkness in their past. The muted sound of the gunshot that had killed her sister echoed in the back of my mind, making me shudder.

"No. It should be just the two of us." But she didn't say why; she just quirked her brow and gave me an expectant look.

Apparently, the discussion was closed, so I figured I'd better suck it up and get to work.

This time, I found my way to her wall much more quickly. I also worked my way through her memories faster, trying not to stay too interested or focused on any one thing. It helped me make better progress, and it also saved me from learning anything else that might haunt me.

When it came to watching her sister get shot again, I still couldn't guard myself against the force of the memory. It was too much, too needlessly violent, too heart wrenching. So I focused on maintaining my control instead. Tears streamed down my face as I worked past that brick in the wall. Birthdays, school days, summers, vacations... I watched all of it stream past until

I finally found myself in a dark space. I didn't want to call it a room, because I could see neither the walls nor the floor. My feet rested on darkness, and it also surrounded me. But somehow, I could see myself clearly, as if some dim, unknown light source hung over my head. I searched for it above me, but there was nothing there.

"Tracy?" I called, not sure what to do or where I was.

She's done it. I heard her, but it was more of an echo than her actual voice. *You've done it*, she corrected.

"Now what?" Just then, a snowplow appeared out of the darkness. I tried to run from it, but it was surprisingly agile. Oddly, it didn't dismember me as I'd expected it would when it literally plowed into me. I landed softly in the front shovel and was pushed back out onto the battlefield, just on the other side of the barbed wire.

I opened my eyes to find her grinning at me. "Now we move on."

"Why did that snowplow work on me? I knew it wasn't real." I paused for a moment. "Actually, that isn't true. It came at me so fast, and my immediate impression was that it was going to kill me. When it didn't, I was so relieved that I let it carry me wherever." I laughed at myself. "You have to teach me some of those added defenses. Apparently, the element of surprise is invaluable."

"Of course. We will start with that tomorrow. Those are things you can constantly change and evolve as you see fit. They're not as important as making sure you keep your wall strong. But they help serve as distractions. Plus, you already know how to effectively push someone out, you know. You did it to me."

"That seems like a long time ago," I said as I sank back into my chair.

"Yes, well, tomorrow we will have some fun. Then the real work starts."

I hate it when she says that, I thought as I made my way to the door.

That night, Owen grilled me on the day's training while the three of us ate dinner. "How did it go?"

I wasn't sure how much detail to give them. Tracy had only requested I not say anything about *her*; she hadn't asked me to keep quiet about how far I'd progressed with my training. But how could I tell them I'd gotten all the way into her mind without divulging what I'd seen there?

Taking a breath to try and calm my internal war, I tried to relax, not sure why I felt so unsettled about the hurdle I jumped. "It went really well." I knew he wouldn't leave it at that, but I hesitated anyway, still searching for the right words.

"Great! And?"

"And, I got all the way into Tracy's mind." I hadn't exactly planned to tell him—at least not yet—but I'd never been too fond of lying.

"You what?" he shouted at me. I glanced around, smiling at the others at the table, trying to encourage them to go back to their own conversations. Mitchell smiled almost approvingly, but he refrained from commenting and shoveled another bite of his salad into his mouth.

Owen leaned in closer and whispered, "You what?"

"You heard me." I stabbed at my noodles instead of making eye contact, suddenly feeling coy. Why should he be so surprised? Hadn't I shown him I could accomplish anything I, well, put my mind to?

"How?" he said, leaning in so close that I could feel his hot breath on my hand as I twirled my spaghetti around my fork.

"That's something even Tracy is struggling to understand. She wants to learn, though—probably so she can teach the rest of you to do it."

He sat back in his chair and nodded, his jealousy—or whatever that had been—passing just as quickly as it had flared up. A smile made itself at home on his face, making my heart leap. It felt good to have that sensation again. "My girl, the prodigy. The only one to hack into Tracy's mind." He nudged Mitchell with his elbow, and our friend nodded at me, raising his glass in a silent toast.

The desire to beam at his compliment was outweighed by my desire to not get flayed by Tracy. "Pipe down, will you?" I snapped.

Lucky for me, all the people around us were still absorbed in their own conversations.

His smile didn't break. "So, now what? Control?"

"She pushed me out of her mind with a freaking snowplow, so I asked her to teach me how to build some extra defenses. I think I need one of those machines in my head."

Mitchell chuckled, and I went on. "Then she said after that, the 'real work' starts."

Owen laughed out loud. "She's right. Control is hard to master. It was a strange task for me. It didn't feel right, controlling someone else." He shrugged, keeping his tone lighthearted. "But it saved my skin more than a few times, so I'm glad I learned it."

Finally, Mitchell chimed in. "Control can be a slippery slope. Make sure you keep your footing."

I wasn't sure what he meant by that, so I decided not to dwell on it. "Well, that'll be for another day. Tomorrow, I beef up my defenses."

"You can do better than a snowplow," Mitchell said without looking up from his plate.

"Like what, Mitch?" I asked.

"Anything you want. Use your imagination." He said it so matter-of-factly and didn't elaborate on my options.

"What's yours like?"

Mitchell smiled out of one side of his mouth. "You'll never have to find out if you know what's good for you."

Owen laughed. "We all know better than to go traipsing through your cobwebs, Mitch. I already feel sorry for the poor sap that tries to get into your head, Mac."

I looked up at him and smiled; he'd already gotten into my head, and without having to scale a fence or deal with death by puppy. Despite the way I'd basically ignored him since Maddie, I couldn't imagine having to go through any of this without him. Maddie's death had ended the burning infatuation that had kept him at the forefront of my mind constantly, but it hadn't snuffed the flame out completely. Instead, it had left slow, burning hot coals that kept me warm at night.

Reaching across the table to grab his hand, I simply said, "Indeed."

The next morning, Tracy started teaching me about building up my defenses, adding traps, and pushing people out. "I don't usually spend special lessons on this, since most people just adapt things they've seen other people do, but I thought we might have fun experimenting with it."

I nodded, and she went on. "Your defenses are only limited by your imagination. Mine have a military feel because that's how I was trained. It's what I respond to best, and where I feel most at home. Yours don't have to look like that."

"Is there anything special I should keep in mind?"

She shrugged. "Your defenses must serve one purpose: keeping intruders out. It doesn't matter how. Fear of harm, confusion, and the feeling of sheer defeat are all capable of repelling your enemies."

The word confusion caught my ear. I didn't care to have some terror-riddled landscape in my head, so the idea intrigued me. My haze could add to the confusion. Despite the fact that I didn't want to keep it around forever, I might as well get good use out of it while it was there.

"But, if I confuse someone badly enough for them to get lost in my head, wouldn't they just remain there indefinitely?"

Tracy nodded. "Assuming you didn't know they were there. But the main point of your defenses is to arm yourself against unknown attacks. You already know how to push someone out. If you confuse them long enough to find them, you should be able to get them out yourself."

"Assuming you know to look for them."

She nodded, and we were quiet for a few moments.

"How are you feeling?" Tracy asked me, changing gears rather abruptly.

"Fine, why?"

"As I told you the other day, I hesitate to enter a grieving mind."

"Why would you have to?"

"To test your new defenses, of course." She thought for a moment. "I'm going to get a third party observer in here. Someone who can talk us through a rescue if needed."

A rescue? I didn't want to hurt her. "Tracy, we don't—" However, she'd already walked out of the room. My mouth dried as I considered all the things that could possibly go wrong that would require a third person to step in and help. The original excitement I felt over this "fun" training day turned to dread as I waited for her to come back.

David came into the room and I swallowed, but my mouth was already so dry, nothing went down. I tried to cough out a greeting, but it came out more like a squawk.

He smiled and sat in the extra chair on Tracy's side of the table as she followed him into the room. "This will be fun, I think. Thank you for inviting me."

I cleared my throat. "I can't believe you have time for something like this."

"Like what?" he asked.

"This... dumb," I filled in.

Tracy took the chair beside David, but he didn't turn to look at her—his gaze was fixed on me, his expression serious. "Training is never dumb, Mackenzie. I'm proud to help you, both as part of the Unseen, and as your father."

The word felt foreign, and he didn't use it much because of that. The fact that he was also my boss added another element of strain to our father-daughter dynamic. The word hung awkwardly in the air, and I wondered how long it would take for us to get over that.

Tracy interjected, easing the tension. "Let's get started."

"Tracy, if this is dangerous for you, I don't want to do it," I said. "Seriously. This was supposed to be something fun, not intense and stressful."

"Who's making it intense and stressful?" she asked, sitting up completely straight in her chair, taking on her normal rigid appearance. "David, are you stressed?"

He shook his head no, and I rolled my eyes, resigned to the fact that neither of them was about to listen to me.

"What do I do?" I finally asked.

"Prepare your defenses and try to keep me out."

"I'll follow Tracy. I will alert you of any problems and let you know if you need to ease up," David filled in.

"Okay, just give me a few minutes," I said, shifting in my chair, still uneasy about this whole venture. *Prepare my defenses.* I pictured the caves Owen had taken me to see. They were so lovely, like nothing I'd ever seen before, let alone in the swamps of Florida. I wondered about the acoustics in the caves, imagining how enchanting and confusing a complex concerto would sound in such an echoey space.

Taking a deep breath, I knew I wasn't going to get any more ready than I was in that moment. I looked at Tracy. "Are you sure we should be doing this?" I asked, giving her one last chance to change her mind. But she didn't answer me. Her eyes were closed, and she'd clearly already gotten to work. David gave me a short nod of reassurance, but then he closed his eyes, apparently following her into my mind.

It was odd to be on the other side of mind reading, to watch them both sit stock-still, knowing they were trying hard to violate my mind as I'd done with Tracy's.

Too soon, I noticed a strained expression on Tracy's face. Beads of sweat were forming on her forehead, and she gripped the arms of her chair much too tightly.

Before I could alert either of them to her physical distress, David opened his eyes. "Mackenzie, push her out. *She's floundering.*"

"How can she be floundering? She's only been poking around for a few seconds."

"Time has no meaning in the space of your mind."

My voice, a high and strained version of itself, mirrored the panic I felt. "But I don't know where she is!"

His eyes were cold and demanding. "Then find her."

The open spaces of my mind were vast, and I wasn't sure where to start my search. Closing my eyes, I took a deep breath and began, fanning out my thoughts to search for anything that didn't belong. I tried to send out a signal to give her something familiar to grasp on to.

"Tracy?" I called out, but my voice echoed oddly inside my own head. She didn't reply, and I had no way of knowing if she could hear me.

The memory of David's words echoed in my mind. She's floundering. I shuddered as I picked up the pace, scouring my mind for her.

She's here somewhere. As long as I find her, she'll be okay, right? None of my defenses could really hurt her, could they? Of course they could. That was what they were designed to do. The thought gave me an even greater sense of urgency.

The problem with delving into a person's mind was that the space inside was both finite—in that it was contained within your skull—and infinite—in that it went on for as far as your imagination allowed. It could take me years to find her if she got herself lost enough.

"Tracy, if you can hear me, stay where you are." *If she keeps wandering, I may never find her. She could die with me seventy years from now.* The thought was horrible enough that I started running, searching desperately for her.

Finally, I felt an unfamiliar presence on the outskirts of my mind and smiled with relief. She hadn't gotten very far after all.

I didn't try to use a snowplow. My method for throwing her out was more like blowing up a balloon. It started small, until it filled my whole mind, leaving no space for anything that didn't belong.

Resisting the urge to enjoy the peace of having my mind to myself again, I opened my eyes and turned to look at Tracy. She was bent forward, holding her head in her hands.

"Thank you," she said, but I wasn't sure who she was addressing.

"Tracy, I am so—"

"An apology isn't necessary," she said from behind her

hands. She peeked out at me warily, looking haggard. My horror must have been obvious, because she gave me a weak smile. "Those are some impressive defenses. Combined with your grief, it makes one hell of a maze. I almost pity the Potestas who decide to try you. Almost."

"What was it like?" I ventured, not sure how much she'd be willing to talk about it at the moment.

She sat back while David held a bottle of water out to her. Smiling at him gratefully, she took a long swallow before she began to speak again. "It was lovely at first. There were these rock formations, almost like I was in a cave. Then the music started playing, giving it the perfect atmosphere. I even sat down for a moment so I could enjoy your lovely creation. But when I started trying to find my way out of there, the music got louder, so loud that it echoed off the cave walls, disorienting me. Then the music turned dark. My feet became heavy with the sadness of it. I lost my will to keep walking. When you found me, I was debating sitting down right there—" she paused, "—forever."

"Holy..." I trailed off, not finishing my exclamation. A myriad of emotions bombarded me in that moment. Fear of what I was, horror at what I'd done... but also pride in what I could do.

"David," she said, turning her gaze to him. "You know this isn't the first time I haven't made it past someone's defenses. It doesn't happen very often, but it does happen. I am human after all." He nodded, and I wasn't sure where she was going with her assertion. Tracy was human, yes, but she was the best of the best at what she did. "But it *is* the first time I haven't made it past a rookie's."

"What does that mean?" I asked.

"It means you're a very formidable foe. And I'm glad you're on our side," she answered, the exhaustion creeping into her voice as she rolled her head around her shoulders, trying to stretch her neck.

David turned to her. "Are you up for training tomorrow?"

"I will be. For now, I'm done for the day." She stood with some effort. "If you'll excuse me, I'm going to lie down for a little while." She looked at me before she left. "Good work today."

She left David and me alone in the room. I thought we were done for the day, but when I stood to follow her, he gestured for me to sit back down.

"A word," he said. My legs collapsed automatically, flouncing me back into the chair I'd just vacated.

"I'm worried about you," he said.

"I'm sorry?" I phrased it like a question, not sure how to respond.

"You need to learn how to handle your grief." He was very matter of fact about it, acting like it was something that should be easy for me.

Anger compressed my lips into a thin line, keeping any sharp comments locked tightly behind them, for once.

"Control is a dangerous and difficult skill. If you don't pull it together, you could hurt someone... or yourself."

My eyes narrowed, seemingly of their own accord. "If that's true, and I'm so out of control, why are you pushing me to do these things?"

He frowned at me, and we sat in a stalemate for several minutes. Finally, I'd had enough.

"Am I free to go?" I asked, hoping the ice in my voice would make him shiver.

It didn't. After he simply nodded, I stormed out. He was the one who'd wanted me to start working and training. He was the one who'd wanted me to contribute so soon. Now he had the nerve to imply I wasn't ready? That I was a danger to myself and others? It was an absolute outrage.

I knew I wasn't ready to start. But David continued to force me to plow forward. But now that it wasn't playing out how he wanted, he had the nerve to put the blame on me? To tell *me* to get *my* shit together?

I was so angry that I nearly collided with Owen in the stairwell. "Whoa, what's wrong? You barreled down on me like a boulder on Indiana Jones."

"Nothing," I said and shook my head. He wouldn't understand. He had made it all too clear that he didn't think I was ready either.

"You're right. There are flames hot enough to melt this staircase flickering in your eyes, but there's clearly nothing wrong."

I rolled my eyes, but I decided to tell him. "David doesn't think I'm ready for the lesson on control."

He frowned, but whatever his personal opinions were—and I had a pretty good idea—he decided to keep them to himself. "What happened today? I thought it was supposed to be defensive training day. Something fun."

"That's not how it turned out," I began, and then I relayed the morning's events. Once I'd told him the whole story, I sank down onto the nearest step, feeling overcome by defeat.

"Maybe David's right," I said in a small voice. "Maybe you're right. But if you are, what is my purpose here? What am I supposed to do with myself?" My voice quavered as I thought of Tracy's haggard expression, all because of me, all because of what I'd done to her.

"I think I was wrong," he said quietly as he took a seat beside me on the stairs. "No, I didn't think you were ready. Honestly, I don't think *you* thought you were ready. But you've become more and more focused every day since returning to training. I haven't had to pry you out of bed in quite a long time. That's a win."

I smiled weakly as I stared at my shoes, and he went on, his voice growing softer, warmer. "You're even smiling again, even if it's just little ones, and even if it doesn't reach your eyes yet. I know it will someday, and I'm willing to wait." Tears filled my eyes, but not from grief or sadness. They were tears of gratitude.

He raised my chin with his hand. "Plus, control is a fun skill. Imagine finding someone who bullied you in middle school. Or that guy who attacked you when Mitchell found you! You could make him pick his nose and eat it in public."

Laughing out loud at that, I pulled away from his hand and swiped at the tear that was trickling down my face. "He probably does that on his own."

Maybe I was ready and maybe I wasn't. Maybe that wasn't the point.

"Life happens whether you're ready or not. It's probably best to just enjoy the ride and try your damnedest to stay in the seat," I said, feeling the weight of Maddie's arm around my shoulder.

"Who said that?" he asked.

I lifted my hand to my shoulder and came up empty. "Maddie."

SEVEN

"**W**e normally do control exercises with other members of the Unseen, so I can keep watch on what's going on and make sure it doesn't get out of control." Tracy paused, and I couldn't help thinking of yesterday's training exercise. I hung my head sheepishly, but if she noticed my reaction, she didn't comment.

"However, I'm not sure I want everyone in the group to know just how powerful you are quite yet," Tracy continued. "I need to understand your methods better before word spreads. Then, I can start teaching the others to do what you do. The more people who know, the quicker the Potestas can find out about you. They have spies everywhere. They already know you're special, but they have no idea what they're in for with you. The longer we can keep that a secret, the better our advantage."

I groaned inwardly, and she must've seen the expression on my face.

"Who did you tell, and how much did you tell them?"

"I didn't tell them anything about you or your secrets. That was the only thing you asked me to keep to myself before." The words came out quickly, as if they might build a wall capable of holding back her anger.

"Who did you tell, and how much did you tell them?" Her

stern tone didn't make me want to hear the question a third time.

"Owen and Mitchell. I just told them I made it past your defenses. All of them."

"No one else." She said it like it was a command, not a request.

I nodded as quickly as I could, and she moved on.

"So, anyway, I've asked—"

I cut her off. "No. Not David." The force of my anger made the words echo in the small room.

She stopped, clearly surprised by my interjection.

"Can't we do this on our own?"

She hesitated, but I pushed. "I know I didn't instill much trust in you yesterday, but this isn't you coming at me, this is me coming at you. That's always gone pretty well in the past."

"Control is a dangerous skill," she started.

"So I've heard." David's warning shaped the words, making them more sarcastic than I'd intended. Lucky for me, Tracy ignored the comment completely.

"It can be an odd feeling, to control someone else. With your history of seeing just how far you can go without asking permission first, I'm not sure it's a good idea for us to try this alone.

I cringed. She was absolutely right. I'd done nothing to warrant her trust. "Please," I pleaded, but then I sighed. "If you feel like you need to have someone else in here, please choose someone besides David. What about Owen or Mitchell? They already know. Or Camden? He seems pretty discreet."

She sighed, taking in my desperation. "What's the problem with David? I thought you might enjoy working with him again. Did something happen after I left?"

My voice hardened of its own accord. "No."

Tracy scoffed. "Clearly."

She frowned, but I could tell her resolve was weakening. After staring at me for a long, silent moment, she said, "I am going to give you a task. You are to do that, and only that. If you push it, there will be consequences for you. No matter how talented you are, you cannot hope to have a future here if the other members of your team can't trust you."

Nodding quickly, I tried to paint my face with the most innocent look I possessed.

Her frown deepened into disapproval. "Do *not* make me regret this, Mackenzie."

I gave her a weak smile, hoping to show her I was grateful for this chance to prove I could be trusted.

"Fine. Let's get started. Controlling someone from within their mind is the easiest, and sometimes safest, way to diffuse a potentially deadly situation. If you're staring down the barrel of a gun, you only have to slip into the attacker's mind to convince them to lower the weapon and walk away.

"However, the method isn't without risks. It takes extreme concentration. And if you're face to face with your attacker, it's dangerous to leave your body vulnerable while you're delving into their mind. Particularly if they're working with an accomplice." She paused, and I wondered if she'd experienced something like that before. After seeing so many of her memories, they were a blur. All except one. You'd think you would know a person well after watching her whole life, but the experience had been fast and overwhelming. It had left me with more questions than answers about what made Tracy *Tracy*.

"You don't have to actually control the person in a puppeteer sort of way. All you have to do is plant an idea. They're much more likely to do what you want if they believe they thought of it first. So be both subtle and specific. Their own ideas and personality will mold your original thought, the same way water and sunlight inspire growth in a growing plant. It can change the outcome drastically if you're not careful.

"What I want you to do first is get me to write a sentence. The sentence can be whatever you, or I, want. Just force me to put pen to paper. Nothing more, nothing less." A piece of paper and pen were already sitting on the table between us.

"A sentence," I repeated.

"That's right. Now get to work."

"Tracy, how exactly do you implant an idea when you're in the middle of the blackness of someone's mind?"

"Ideally, with subtlety. Some people just whisper a command and hope it takes, others try something a bit more actionable, like creating a false memory. As always, you need to see what works for you."

Taking a deep breath, I closed my eyes and made my way through her defenses. It felt like it took me forever, but each time I walked through her battlefield and up to her wall, it got a little easier.

Finally, I found myself in the dark space once again. *Plant an idea*, I thought. Easy enough, right? But how was I supposed to plant an idea? It wasn't like I could be literal about it. There weren't any gardening supplies in the expanse of darkness that surrounded me. Or, if there were, I couldn't see them.

Then there was the problem of what I should have her write. *I see your mind*. No, too creepy. *Hey Tracy*. Not thoughtful enough. Then I had it.

With no other ideas for how to *plant an idea*, I shouted the phrase desperately into the darkness. I thought my desperation might give her some urgency. That done, I waited. I couldn't tell if anything was happening, so I shouted it again. Still no visible change, so I decided to open my eyes and reassess the situation. Maybe she could give me some tips on what I was doing wrong, or how I might go about the assignment differently.

Tracy was holding the paper in her hands and staring blankly ahead, as if she'd been reading it. She put it down so I could see, but she didn't look at me.

Are you writing this, or am I? was scrawled messily on the page. Twice.

"That must've been you. My handwriting isn't that messy," I said, trying to lighten the mood. But she only blinked.

"What an odd experience," she said, her voice sounding distant, as if her mind was still someplace else.

"You've never been controlled before?"

"No. I've done it to others, dozens of times. But that..." She trailed off.

Folding my arms over my chest, I felt very proud of what I had done. I had controlled the uncontrollable. "So, how was it?"

"Uncomfortable." She slouched a little in her chair and leaned heavily on the table.

I opened my mouth, but the words didn't come. Uncomfortable wasn't the word I'd expected. In the back of my mind, I'd hoped she might express some pride in my accomplishment. I hadn't taken the time to consider what my accomplishment might have done to her. Then my mind jumped to the most probable ways control would be used against the enemy.

"Have you ever made someone do anything..." I paused, not sure how to finish that sentence.

"Unsavory?" she asked, and then nodded once.

I didn't want to know, and I was suddenly thankful for the fact that most of her memories were now a blur in my mind. I didn't want an image like that—of her questioning someone forcefully, or worse—to color my opinion of her. Anyway, I had no idea how I would react in a similar high-stakes scenario, so I felt like I had no right to judge her.

"Tracy, can I ask you something?" She looked at me, and I noticed her face had started to turn a pale shade of green, almost like she might be sick at any moment.

She nodded and swallowed hard.

"Is... what you did the kind of thing you and David have in mind for me?"

Her eyes cleared a bit, and some of her resolve seemed to return. "I don't know. We're relying on you to save the world and crush the Potestas, so whatever that entails is what you'll be expected to do."

I slumped in my seat. "Is that all?"

She laughed out loud, and the abruptness of the unexpected sound startled me. "Relax. I'm kidding. Don't you know a joke when you see one?" The smile on her face seemed to bring some normal color back into her cheeks. Although she still looked a little pale, she wasn't so green anymore.

"Not from you," I said, a bit indignant.

Despite the sweat on her forehead, she was sitting a little straighter, as if the bad feelings from being controlled were draining from her. Frankly, I was glad it had passed so quickly.

"You will be expected to be part of this team, nothing more, nothing less. You won't be made to do something that makes you uncomfortable, but you are expected to contribute."

"I am ready to contribute. I'm tired of being a mooch, nothing but a gray cloud hanging around here. I want to get out, start working."

"Good, because your first real-world assignment is being handed down tomorrow."

EIGHT

I bounded out of the training room, a ball of excitement and nerves. Owen stood from the machine he'd been using and caught me in his arms. He smelled of sweat and masculinity, and a familiar pulse of desire zinged through me.

"I take it today went better than yesterday?" he said as we spun around in the middle of the gym, surrounded by clanging workout machines and people sparring. A few of them glanced our way and gave us knowing smiles.

I forgot my haze for long enough to plant a kiss on Owen's lips. At first, he was too surprised to respond, but soon, he was kissing me back with abandon, apparently trying to make up for the last few weeks. Someone across the gym started hooting, and we reluctantly pulled apart.

"Wow, what brought that on?" he asked, for only me to hear. "Whatever it was, I think I like it."

"I'm getting my first real-world assignment tomorrow." It felt foreign to say the words out loud. I wasn't a kid anymore. I had a real job, and I'd start work in the morning. Real work—not busywork. Just like that, I'd experienced my own personal coming-of-age.

"Really?" he said softly, rubbing his forehead as if he'd just come down with a headache.

The change in his mood startled me. "What?"

"I just…"

I waited impatiently for him to spit it out. "You just what? Don't think I can do it? Or is it just that you still don't think I'm ready?" My insecurities were showing, and I didn't like it.

He frowned. "No. And frankly, I would love for you to get more assignments if they all result in kisses like that." He forced a smile.

I stuck out my chin, refusing to relent. "Well, what is it then?"

"I don't want you to get hurt."

It struck me as funny because it was just about the last thing I expected him to say, and I stifled a laugh. "I don't think I will, Owen. They won't send me to do something super dangerous on my first mission."

"Do you know anything about it yet?"

"No. I'm supposed to get my orders tomorrow."

"Well, you're mine until then," he said. There was an air of seduction in his voice, and the twinkle in his eyes returned.

Trying to encourage this more positive, though rather sudden change in mood, I asked, "What did you have in mind?" When I smiled back at him, I realized it felt genuine. It was a good sensation.

After Owen got cleaned up, we headed to dinner together. Most of the Unseen were gathered in the dining room at the same time for once, and Owen banged his fork on his soda can. "Excuse me, everyone. Tomorrow, our little Mac gets her first real assignment. She's leaving the nest."

I felt my cheeks flush amidst the chorus of hoots and hoorays from the group.

"So, tonight, we celebrate her initiation."

My stomach dropped as I wondered what exactly he meant by initiation. "Oh, jeez guys, you don't have do to that," I said, hoping to save myself some embarrassment.

I gave Mitchell a hopeful glance, but he shook his head. "No fighting it. They do this for everyone. No matter what." Turning back to his plate, he shoveled more food into his mouth, but the corners of his mouth had twisted into a smile. *Traitor.*

Camden ran into the pantry and emerged with a tiara and a plastic lei necklace. After I put them on—mostly to shut everyone up—a few of the guys came over and lifted up my chair to bounce me around the dining room. Everyone laughed and clapped as they sang songs of encouragement and good luck. It was a pep rally, just for me. It was terrifying, but a laugh or two escaped my lips in spite of myself.

By the time they set me back down, almost everyone was done eating.

"Now it's time to play truth or dare," Owen said.

"What? No," I said. True, I'd learned to block my thoughts, but it still didn't seem like the best game to play with a group of mind readers.

"Aw, come on. Everyone plays. It's fun," he pleaded.

"It never gets awkward, serious, or ruined by the fact that you all know who's lying and who's not?" I folded my arms over my chest, knowing I couldn't possibly be wrong.

"No! Come on, we're all good sports, and we know better than to pry. Justine learned that the hard way when she got tangled up in Kyle's defenses—standing naked in front of a crowd of people, trying to give a speech." Everyone laughed, but it still didn't hold much appeal for me. "Just try it. We do it with all the first timers," Owen explained.

I looked at Mitchell, who nodded and shrugged. "My first time, they made me try to balance eggs on my feet while I did a handstand. Needless to say, we needed more eggs by the end of the night."

I laughed. Maybe this *would* be fun. "Fine. But I go first."

"Fair enough," Owen said.

As soon as I'd said it, I regretted it though. I didn't know what to ask, or who to ask it of. I looked at Camden, full of joy, despite his imposing size.

"Camden, truth or dare?"

"Dare." His deep voice resonated throughout the dining room.

"I dare you to squeeze into the cupboard under the sink."

"C'mon, Mac, can't I use one of the cupboards where the sink *doesn't* take up forty percent of the real estate?"

"Sure. That's fair. Now go," I said, pulling out my cell phone to document his struggle.

We all cried with laughter as our six-foot-six friend valiantly tried—and failed—to cram himself into the biggest kitchen cupboard we had. The kitchen—and Camden—would never be the same. The game only went downhill from there. They dared me to share my most embarrassing story, so I found myself telling them about one of my open-mike performances with Maddie. Two things had gone wrong that night—I got the hiccups halfway through the set, and thanks to a poor wardrobe choice, I inadvertently flashed the entire audience in the intense overhead lighting. Maddie had thought it was hilarious, so she hadn't told me my high beams were on until later.

I made the others do ridiculous things and tell equally embarrassing stories. My face was starting to hurt from all the laughter.

Before I knew it, someone was passing out mugs of hot chocolate, and we were all calming down.

"Now, it's everyone's turn to tell Mac about their first assignments," Owen said.

"Ooh, I like this idea," I said, eager to get some insight into what I might expect for the coming days.

But their tales were all so different. Camden told me about a local teacher he'd been assigned to check out. Turned out the guy was planning to bomb the school because he'd received another bad evaluation. That one turned my stomach a bit.

Mitchell's was the most surprising. He'd been assigned to a college girl. The higher-ups thought she was a possible suicide bomber, but it turned out she was just a suicide risk. She wasn't involved with the Potestas, and she wasn't a reader. Mitchell kept a lot of the details to himself, but something in his tone said he'd cared more about her than he was letting on. Before I could ask what happened to her, the group moved on.

The others shared their tales of success and failure—each

fascinating in its own right—and Owen went last.

"Mine is probably the most embarrassing."

"I can attest to that. I'm surprised David kept you on after that foul up," Mitchell said, and Owen threw his empty mug at him. As if expecting the attack, Mitchell caught it one-handed.

"You have to understand," Owen said to me. "The assignment was to follow a blonde, fourteen-year-old girl whose primary interest was hanging out at the mall. Her name was Tiffany. Do you know how many fourteen-year-old blonde girls named Tiffany frequent the mall?"

"A kid? Why were you following a kid?" I asked, not sure I wanted the answer. The last thing I wanted to hear was that I might be asked to attack a child.

"Apparently, David thought she was a possible target for the Potestas. I was supposed to find out why—you know, if she needed protection if they intended to forcibly recruit her. It was a fact-finding mission."

I nodded, feeling a little better.

"Anyway, as you can probably guess, I followed the wrong girl all day long, listening to her drone on about clothes, boys, and bands. It was horrible. Never once did it occur to me that there were no Potestas anywhere around her, and she had no memory of meeting one of them. David was not pleased."

I laughed, enjoying the levity of the moment. As I looked around at the smiling faces that surrounded me, I felt a sense of peace. Although my life had been shattered, I could probably make something from the pieces.

At the end of the night, Owen walked me to my room. A note was taped to my door, but I ignored it as we stood facing each other, our hands still entwined.

"Thank you," I told him.

"For what? Initiating you? We do that for everyone. It's fun." He shrugged.

"For everything." I leaned in and kissed him slowly, deeply. Emotions and hormones I wasn't yet ready for flared to life, so I pulled away before either of us was through.

He cleared his throat. "I guess I better say goodnight." Then he lifted one hand and gently caressed the side of my face. "I won't say this isn't hard, Mac, but you're worth it." With that, he turned and left.

"Goodnight," I said to his back. He gave me a jaunty wave over his shoulder. *He's too good for you.* It had become a recurrent thought lately, but I pushed it away as I turned to pull the note off my door.

Meet in my office at 8 am to receive your orders.

— David.

A sinking feeling settled in my stomach at the prospect of an early-morning meeting with David. After the way we'd parted yesterday, I hadn't really thought about what it would be like to see him again. Not to mention everything that had happened since our last talk. He hadn't really been in the forefront of my mind.

Top it off with the fact that he made me feel like an out of control, ill prepared child, and I didn't really want to waste any brain cells on the matter.

Crumpling the note, I tossed it into the trash can next to my bed and debated what to do. I could either be responsible and go to the meeting a few minutes early to give us time to clear the air, or I could go right on time, get my orders, and leave.

As I got myself ready for bed, trying to calm the jitters coming from all corners of my mind—excitement and nerves over the new job, dread over meeting David, and the ever-present haze of grief—I decided on a civil but cold approach with David. After all, if he wanted to treat me like the child in this relationship, he could be the adult and make the first move.

I turned off the light and settled into bed, wondering exactly what I would have to do. No matter what it was, the next morning would be the first day of my new life. No more living in the haze, no more looking back. Nope, it was time to pick up the pieces; it was time to fight back.

Promptly at 8 am, I arrived at David's office. I think Owen noticed my jitters, but he probably assumed they were from the assignment, not meeting with David. I hadn't mentioned our tiff to him, so he had no idea we weren't on good terms. He probably would have scolded me for disrespecting the boss. But he had some bizarre hero-worship thing going on with David that I didn't share. He was just a guy who happened to be my dad... and because of that very fact, he'd made some decisions with pretty direct consequences on my life. He seemed pretty dang human to me.

In the end, Owen simply wished me luck, assured me I'd be great, and kissed me lightly before I took a deep breath and ventured into the lion's den, unsure if I would play the role of the lion or the intruder.

David sat at his desk, and Tracy was in one of the chairs across from him. It was becoming a familiar picture.

"Good morning," David said, his tone unreadable.

"Morning," I answered, nodding at Tracy. She nodded back. Taking a seat, I spied a familiar file on David's desk.

"Isn't that the scientist's file?" I asked.

"Yes. He is your assignment," David said.

"But I thought we decided he wasn't a threat."

"You decided that. I believe he warrants observation." He didn't elaborate, so I pushed him.

"On what grounds? Because he studies dangerous chemicals?"

"Yes." Somehow, he'd ended up adopting up my cold yet civil tactic before I could.

"We've received intel that the Potestas may be interested in him. We need to know why, and what's going on. You leave for Michigan in three hours. Tracy is going to accompany you to supervise and offer any guidance you might need. Pack a bag for at least two days. I expect a full report upon your return."

Looking at Tracy, I thought of the training she'd be missing while she was basically babysitting me. "I think it's a waste of resources."

David looked straight into my eyes, "I hope you're right."

He paused to let that sink in. "Good luck, and get going. You have a plane to catch."

I didn't have much time to obsess over what the no-nonsense meeting with David meant. When David had said we were leaving in three hours, he'd meant our flight was departing at that time, not that we would have to leave the facility in three hours. I rushed upstairs and packed a bag, hoping I wasn't forgetting anything vital, and barely got to kiss Owen and nod at Mitchell before Tracy whisked me off to the airport.

I didn't say goodbye to David, which felt odd, despite our circumstances. He was my father, and it would be several days before I saw him again. Seemed like there should've been some kind of fare well.

"I should've said goodbye to David."

"There wasn't really time." She was so matter of fact about it—like it didn't make a difference that I hadn't said a kind word to my father before I left on a potentially dangerous mission. Okay, that was dramatic, but still, it was true.

The airport was only about twenty minutes from the facility, and we were still tight on time, so my concerns about David were whisked away by the bustle of the airport.

"David could've asked us to meet him at seven," I grumbled. "It would have given us more time." I was still stewing about my rushed goodbye with Owen, not to mention my nonexistent goodbye with David as Tracy kept a brisk pace toward the security line.

Rather than acknowledge my statement or respond in any way, she kept her eyes on the target ahead. That was fine with me. Nothing she could say would change our circumstances or ease the stress of the situation.

Besides, the pace she was keeping was enough to make me breathless before too long, so any additional conversation was impossible.

We didn't have any bags to check, so that helped, and they were boarding by the time we got to the gate, so we just walked right onto the plane.

Once seated, I took a few moments to catch my breath.

"You're out of shape," Tracy said. "You should keep up with the workout regimens."

"I do! And yet, it's still hard to keep pace with you in a crowd," I muttered as I leaned my head back against the seat and waited for my heart rate to go from sprint run to resting.

"I like it that way." She made no effort to hide her smile.

I shook my head and leaned forward to grab the file on the scientist. Figured I might as well get some studying done on the way. The flight took off while I attempted another read through of his articles about separating chemicals and isolating the most dangerous toxins, but I got frustrated about halfway through the flight. It might as well have been moon language for all the meaning I was able to take away.

Exasperated, I closed the file and jammed it back into my backpack. "Tracy, I don't know how much help I'm going to be. I don't even understand what this guy is studying. If his mind is anything like these papers, I'm not going to understand a single one of his thoughts. I'm not a chemist. I'm a music therapist."

"No." She lowered her voice and glanced at the people sitting near us. "You are Unseen. Identifying potential dangers isn't about understanding their specific fields, although that can be helpful. It's about understanding people—what motivates them, and what they intend to do with the resources available to them."

I sat back in my seat, trying to find some comfort in her words. But David's last words to us haunted me. Why would he want *me* to be right? Unless he was genuinely worried that this guy was bad news… but if that were the case, why would he send his daughter into a potentially dangerous situation?

I still didn't have any answers when the plane landed, though I had plenty of remaining questions. As we disembarked, Tracy checked her watch. "One thirty. We've missed his lunch hour. He gets off at five, and then he goes straight to a café for a cup of coffee after work."

Based on what I'd seen online and in his file, the man's personal life was nonexistent. Never married, no kids, estranged from his parents, and no siblings. Lots of people had bad relationships with their families, of course, but maybe it was David's sign of something amiss?

The cold Michigan air bit into me the instant we stepped outside to get the car, freezing the air in my lungs, making me cough. I wrapped my arms around my body, tucking the coat Tracy had loaned me for the trip closer to my skin.

"Good Lord. We couldn't have been given an assignment in a more tropical part of the world?"

"We live in a more tropical part of the world," Tracy said, deadpan as ever as she buckled her seat belt.

"Touché." I rubbed my hands together, trying to warm them up after the short trek to the car. "I hope we don't have to spend much time outside for this one."

"Suck it up. Your thin Florida blood could use some thickening anyway," she said.

"Yeah, yeah."

As Tracy drove to the university, I scanned the file again. It didn't reveal much. Dr. Jeppe lived in a small apartment near the university. In addition to his post-work cup of coffee, he began his mornings with a cup of joe at the café. He spent most of his weekends working or delivering lectures, which helped explain why he was single. Who would want to date someone who never had time to be together? I wondered if he even cared. From his very impressive resume, it seemed to me that he was married to his work... and that was how he liked it.

We arrived at the university long before the scientist's workday was over, so we staked out the campus a little, hoping to catch a glimpse of the man we were there to watch. We planned to make a sneak attack on his mind later, at the coffee shop. It was exhilarating to be out on a real job, even if I was just supposed to gauge whether this guy was a threat.

We never did catch sight of him, so at four thirty, we headed over to the café listed in the file so we could ensure we had a seat when the professor arrived. If he left on time, he would be there at five fifteen. It would be my first opportunity to delve into his mind.

We ordered drinks and took a seat in the back corner of the

café. It was a cute little spot with outdoor seating, but it was way too cold for anyone to take advantage of it. Part of me already longed for home, milder temperatures, and Owen's warm embrace. But the rest of me knew I needed to stay focused.

I'd never spent many nights away from home, Maddie's house notwithstanding. The woman who'd raised me, Amanda, never took me anywhere, and she avoided spending recreational time with me like it would've killed her. Since I hadn't been a performance major, I never even traveled to competitions with school.

"I think this is the first legitimate trip I've ever taken." I addressed the words as much to myself as to Tracy.

"How old are you again?"

My back straightened, and I held my head high. "Twenty-five."

"That's a quarter of a century mostly wasted, if you ask me. You need to get out more."

Tracy couldn't help but tell it like it was; I couldn't help but laugh.

At five o'clock, Tracy ran through the scenario one last time. "When he comes in, you get to work. I'll do what I can to ensure you have a safe space to do your job. If you encounter any problems, get out, and we'll try again in the morning."

I nodded, searching restlessly for Dr. Jeppe. Each time the bell over the door jangled, my heart raced. And each time it wasn't him, I swallowed my disappointment and kept right on looking.

After what felt like an eternity, I saw him walk through the front door. He didn't go to the counter and order his drink. Instead, the barista called out a greeting to him as he took a seat at his usual table, which we had strategically stationed ourselves next to. "Afternoon, Dr. Jeppe. Your coffee will be ready soon."

Rather than acknowledge the greeting in any way, he buried his face in some paperwork. I could only assume it was work related. Tracy cleared her throat, signaling me to get to work.

Leaning back in my chair, I shut my eyes, hoping I looked like I was just resting for a moment.

As I reached out for his mind, I was immediately met with a problem. Walking through the darkness, I stepped onto a spring trap that launched me out of his mind. I opened my eyes and gasped in surprise.

Tracy eyed me as I glanced around, hoping I hadn't drawn too much attention to myself. No one seemed to be watching, thankfully, and the doctor was still consumed by his work.

He has defenses, I thought to her as I tried to calm my racing heart. If he were truly a run-of-the-mill scientist, he wouldn't have any need to protect his mind. He wouldn't even know such a thing was possible or necessary. It meant he was either a mind reader or working with one.

Tracy frowned. *Well, you know how to get past defenses. Find out why he has them.*

Frowning right back at her, I gave her a sidelong glance before closing my eyes and venturing out again. This time, I was prepared, so I adjusted my approach accordingly.

I set off the spring trap again, but it didn't affect me this time. After all, it wasn't real, and the element of surprise—the only thing the trap had going for it—was gone. There was a barrage of additional defenses, including a box that fell from above to apparently trap an intruder and what appeared to be a minefield. However, I wasn't sure because I never set any of them off. I just saw the lumps in the ground. There was also a pit covered with leaves and foliage. All in all, it was pretty uninventive.

Until I got to his wall. It was immense, and it stretched out before me, seemingly extending forever. It was nothing like Tracy's wall. Hers seemed to go on for infinity too, but this… I paused as I looked at it, struggling to define it. It was infinite, but it was also empty. There was no sign of any memories embedded within it.

How can that be? I wondered as I leaned in closer.

But I didn't get to examine it to my heart's content. Suddenly, I was jerked away from the wall and rather unceremoniously plopped back in myself.

Blinking at Tracy, I asked, "What happened?"

She nodded toward the target, and I saw him leaving the

café, coffee in hand.

"I—"

She cut me off. "Not here." And with that, she stood and walked back to our car, never once looking back to ensure I was following her. Scrambling to my feet, I struggled to decode the strange scene I'd just witnessed while also keeping pace with Tracy. I stumbled on the way to the car, but I played it off as if I'd slipped on an ice patch, and I nodded gratefully to the passerby who helped me up.

Before I knew it, Tracy and I were sitting together in the car, but I was a little afraid to speak. Tracy was stone faced as she stared straight ahead, navigating the car toward our hotel. I took the opportunity to try and sort through what had happened, and what it might mean. Obviously, David had been at least partially right. There was just cause to suspect Dr. Jeppe. Otherwise, why would those defenses be in place? They seemed so weak, almost artificial, with the exception of that wall.

Silently, Tracy drove to the hotel where we'd be staying, and I trailed her as she checked in at the desk. We didn't exchange a word until she secured the locks on the door of our room and sat on the bed across from where I'd absently seated myself.

"Tell me what happened."

"His defenses were odd," I said, rubbing my forehead. "Almost insincere."

"What do you mean by that?" she asked.

"Well, it was too easy to get past them. Like he didn't have any stake in them working."

That gave Tracy pause, but she didn't comment. "Go on."

"His wall, on the other hand... well, I'm not sure how to bypass it. It wasn't like yours or mine. There didn't seem to be any way around, above, or through it."

Tracy's expression seemed confused, so I took a breath, trying to gather my thoughts.

"Our walls are made from memories. Although there are a million or more of them, our memories are limited to our personal experiences. Eventually, inevitably, there is an end. Everyone has a first memory, right? Well, Dr. Jeppe's wall is made up of... nothing. And nothingness can potentially stretch on for-ever." I flopped back onto the bed, absorbing what I'd just said. How on Earth was I supposed to get inside this guy's head? Suddenly, my seemingly mundane task was becoming much more of a challenge than I'd anticipated.

"Do you think you could come with me in the morning? Maybe you could identify his wall, help me understand what to do."

She shook her head. "You need a lookout; someone to make sure nothing is amiss. The fact that he has defenses is extremely unexpected, and it's all the more reason for us to be on our guard."

That night, as I lay in an unfamiliar bed, staring up at an unfamiliar ceiling, I found it hard to relax. I tried not to despair, despite the fact that I felt like I was failing at my first job, but trying was definitely different from doing.

Clearly, there was more to Dr. Jeppe than met the eye, and I'd missed it from the first. Perhaps if I'd been more prepared, I would've had a better idea of what to do at this stage. As far as I knew, he wasn't a reader. So what could explain his wall of nothing? How and why had he formed such seemingly iron-clad defenses? I continued to circle back to those questions as sleep evaded me.

My emotions ran wild as I flounced onto my side, willing myself to sleep even as I raged at the situation.

"Stop it. I'm trying to sleep," Tracy called out from the next bed.

"Stop what? I know I wasn't snoring."

"You're huffing and tossing and turning. Whatever you think you did wrong, it doesn't matter. Settle down. You need your rest."

"But—"

"It doesn't matter. Tomorrow does. And I'd like to get it right this time so we can go home and get out of this freezing, godforsaken state. So go to sleep. I'll blame you if we have to stay here another night."

Settle down, I thought. But how could I possibly do that? My fingers twitched. In that moment, I needed music. I did something I hadn't done in a very long time. I got up, dug my iPod out of my backpack, and let Gaspard deal with my worries.

The music surrounded me with its familiar notes. And although Maddie didn't come with them, that was ok. This was different. This wasn't about finding her. It was about finding focus. And Gaspard de la Nuit had never let me down in that department.

Before the end of the piece, I drifted off, carried into the depths of my own mind by Ravel's work.

NINE

The next morning, Tracy and I chose a different table at the coffee shop, farther away from the scientist's normal spot, in an effort to go unnoticed. We sat across from each other, silently scheming. For what had to be the fifth time, she stressed the importance of getting in and out of the professor's mind as quickly as possible. I nodded as our target came through the door, perfectly on schedule.

This time, I zeroed in on him and immediately made my way to the wall of nothing. It made a hollow glass sound when I knocked on it. Admittedly, I was a little disappointed when my hand made contact. Secretly, I hoped my hand would just pass through it, and this defense would prove to be like the others—artificial and unimpressive.

Looking back at some of the other traps, I wondered if I could use something from within his mind to break down the wall. I walked back to the hole, haphazardly covered with brush and debris, searching for a stick wide enough to do some damage. Finally, I found one I hoped was suitable, but when I tried to pick it up, my hand passed through it.

Of course it did. The stick isn't real, you idiot.

Frustrated, I went back to his wall, considering my options, knowing time was ticking away as I debated what to do. The professor could very well leave the coffee shop before I made any progress. With no other ideas, I took off my left shoe. To my relief, I was able to hold it in my hand. I suspected that it worked because I'd brought it, along with the rest of my clothes, into Dr. Jeppe's mind, which made it more real to me.

At first, I merely tapped the wall with the heel of my boot, afraid of the consequences, although I couldn't imagine what they might be. If Jeppe discovered me, I knew he wouldn't be thrilled about my presence, and that was the only motivation I needed to work quietly. But it had no effect, except for a pleasant little glass 'ting' sound. I hit a little harder, slowly increasing my force until I was all-out pounding on his wall, the sound resonating through the landscape around me. Soon, the wall began to crack.

But before I could bring it down, I felt the tug. *No*, I thought. *He must be getting up*. I fought to stay in his mind, doubled down on my focus, and continued pounding his wall with my shoe, until it finally came crashing down around me. I skittered away from it, trying to shield myself from the falling shards of glass, despite the fact that I was wearing several layers and probably wasn't in any danger at all.

Sweating from the effort, I wondered if I was actually perspiring in my seat across from Tracy. I could only hope I wasn't showing any visible distress.

Grateful for my long sleeves, I brushed the glass from my arms and made my way through the mess I'd created inside Dr. Jeppe's mind. As soon as I made my way inside, I knew he wasn't a reader. His thoughts were scattered and disorganized, and his memories were too easily accessed, just out in the open for anyone to collect as they saw fit. It didn't take long for me to find the information I needed.

Dux Ducis is really putting the pressure on. His voice was higher and more unsure than I'd expected it would be. He seemed frightened in this memory. *I'm beginning to regret agreeing to explore this avenue.*

Who is Dux Ducis? I wondered, dreading to go further down the rabbit hole.

But I delved deeper into Jeppe's memories anyway, searching for the moment he'd met Dux Ducis. I needed to find out who he was, not to mention what he wanted Jeppe to do. Unfortunately, their first contact seemed to have happened via email, not in person. Dux Ducis had introduced himself as an interested benefactor and asked him how far he could take his research with proper funding. At first, Jeppe had been excited. But then, the threats started arriving. They were on a tight deadline, and Jeppe wasn't making the kind of progress this Dux Ducis wanted to see. One note even threatened that the work would be tested on Jeppe if he didn't deliver, and fast.

It wasn't clear how Dux Ducis found Jeppe's cell phone number—his e-mail address was easily accessible to anyone with Google, but his cell phone was unlisted. Still, found it he had. The threats and sensitive information all arrived via text messages on his phone. He'd never even heard Dux Ducis' voice.

I ignored the sense of dread building in the back of my mind, with Dux Ducis at the root of it. Something sinister was going on, but I wasn't sure if I'd be able to figure it out—and prove it—in time to put a stop to it.

All right, so I don't know who this guy is. But maybe I can find out what he wants Jeppe to do. I continued to move ahead, searching for clues as to the nature of their arrangement. What I saw next would be burned into my memory for the rest of my days.

I found myself in a lab with white walls and oak-colored cabinets. Dr. Jeppe was dressed in his white lab coat, pushing his glasses up higher on his nose with a hand covered in a blue glove that went up to his elbow. He stood in front of an island—on one side there was a sink. Arranged on the white countertop in the middle were a recording device, some papers, and a laptop. He turned the recorder on and started talking. "I've successfully combined three of the four toxins into a gas. Today will be the first live test of the substance." He moved over to a glass box.

"Subjects are two primates, most similar in lung capacity to humans. Additional testing will be done on pigs, to monitor possible skin reactions."

My instinct to pull away from this memory was overwhelming as dread deepened in the pit of my stomach. But I had to know what Jeppe and now Dux Ducis were doing, so I stayed put. The chimps were cleaning each other, totally unaware of the fate that awaited them. Although I didn't know what was coming either, I knew it wouldn't be good.

Dr. Jeppe moved over to a pump set up outside the glass box. "The test begins now, at oh nine hundred hours on September 15, 2014." He flipped a switch on the pump, and it hummed to life.

Soon, the box filled with smog, and the chimps started to scream. It was the most horrifying sound I'd ever heard in my life. Everything about it—the pitch and length of the cries, the sheer desperation of the sound—told me they were dying and they were afraid.

Although I knew it was ridiculous, one of the chimps looked right at me, its brown eyes pleading for help. I reached out for it, but this was just a memory, and I was helpless to change it.

Before long, big chunks of fur started falling off the chimps, blood poured from their eyes, and their screaming was interrupted by bouts of coughing that led to spurts of bloody vomit. I squeezed my eyes shut, not wanting to see any more of their suffering.

After entirely too long, the chimps fell silent. I heard Dr. Jeppe's voice and peeked out of one eye to see what he was doing. He watched the chimps without emotion, typing notes into his computer. "Upon initial observation, the toxin seems quite effective. Subjects appear to be deceased after only four minutes and thirty-eight seconds of exposure. Adding the fourth toxin may speed the process."

The fourth toxin? It was all too much. I finally pulled myself out of his mind, desperate to escape.

When I opened my eyes, I realized I was drenched in sweat. I dared to glance over at Dr. Jeppe, who was looking at his watch with a confused and flustered expression on his face. He quickly gathered his things and rushed out of the café.

Leaning forward on the table, I rested my head on my folded arms "I think I'm going to be sick," I whispered.

"Not here," Tracy said, totally unsympathetic to my plight. She stood up and kicked the back of my chair, apparently encouraging me to follow her.

It took everything I had to keep it together long enough to get outside, where I leaned on a handicapped parking sign and left my breakfast on the pavement.

Tracy took me by the arm and ushered me over to—and then into—the car, which was parked a short distance away, before I could even wipe my mouth. Once seated in the passenger seat, I immediately started shaking. Moments later, Tracy started the car and glanced at me.

"Nope. Not here. Hey." She paused, waiting for a response, but I didn't give her one. I kept hearing the otherworldly shrieks of the chimps. I clapped my hands over my ears to try and block them out. As I thought about what I'd seen, not to mention the toxin's potential effects on humans, bile rose again in the back of my throat.

"Hey!" Tracy yelled, forcing me to look at her. "Keep it together. You're stronger than this."

I shook my head, tears springing to my eyes. No, I wasn't stronger than this, and I certainly wasn't strong enough to deal with this scientist. Chimps were just animals, but watching them suffer like that... I could only imagine how I would have felt if I'd seen him torture people.

Owen was right. There was pure evil out there, and I couldn't even begin to comprehend it. Disappointment and regret blanketed my heart. I should have never taken the job with the Unseen. I was ill equipped.

I was so busy thinking about the screaming, bleeding chimps, I didn't even realize we'd made it back to the hotel.

Tracy led me into our room and helped me sit on my bed. Then she knelt in front of me and stared into my tear-filled eyes. "Pull it together, Mac." She grabbed hold of my chin and shook my face a little—not hard, just enough to get me to look at her. "I mean it."

After I took a deep, shuddering breath, she nodded at me.

"Good. Now, tell me what happened."

I couldn't. I couldn't talk about it right then. Saying the words out loud made them real. I'd been so very wrong about the scientist. But then the memory of what he'd said about the chimps' lungs being similar to a human's echoed in my head, and I knew I had to be strong. I had to force myself to do what needed to be done. Flying up off the bed, I accidently caught Tracy in the chin with my knee. "We have to talk to David. We need to warn him."

TEN

Tracy and I didn't speak much on the way home. She must've opted to let me work through the ordeal on my own. Or perhaps she was off in her own world, trying to puzzle out what I'd seen and what should be done about it.

Luckily, she was able to get a flight out pretty quickly, so we got home in the early afternoon.

Tracy had called David from the airport in Michigan to tell him we were on our way home. Their conversation was brief, and no details were exchanged. I didn't know if that was normal protocol, or if it was because I hadn't shared many details with Tracy. The echo of the chimps' screaming kept me from dwelling on it too long.

On the drive back to the facility, she finally spoke. "Tell me something, Mackenzie."

Failing to acknowledge her, I watched the greenery of my home state zip past us.

"How did you keep him there?"

That was enough to get me to look at her. "What?"

"At the time he would normally leave, he stood halfway up, but then his face took on a confused expression and he sat back down. He'd already finished his coffee and read the paper, but he stared down at the newsprint anyway, holding his cup in his hand. Then, as soon as you opened your eyes, he seemed to come back to himself. He flew out of the café, obviously late for work."

I tried to make sense of what she was telling me. "When I was at his wall, I felt the tug of him leaving. But I hadn't gotten into his head yet. So I just said no, but I wasn't necessarily talking to him. I wasn't consciously trying to control him; I just wanted to get the job done."

"I see." Her tone indicated she was a little taken aback by my answer, and frankly, so was I.

"If I stay, I need a lot more training, Tracy. I can't just run around unconsciously controlling people. That's kind of dangerous, isn't it?"

But she ignored my question. "What do you mean, *if* you stay?" The alarm in her voice was unmistakable.

"I don't think I'm cut out to be such an active member of the Unseen. Maybe I can do paperwork or something more behind the scenes? Owen tried to warn me about the evil out there, and so did you. But I can't handle it." I stared out the window, but instead of the passing landscape, I saw the chimp's big, brown eyes staring at me through the glass of his prison. I shut my eyes. "I've let you down."

She chuckled, which wasn't exactly the response I was expecting. "That's ridiculous. You haven't even shared the nature of what you learned with me, but I can already tell this mission was a complete success. You've done your job, and you've done it splendidly. What more could we ask for?"

"For me to not be emotionally shattered by the job." Hysteria surfaced again, and I practically shouted the words at her.

She glanced at me and frowned, then stared straight ahead as she guided the car back to our home. "That will come," she said after a moment, her voice uncharacteristically hushed.

But maybe I didn't want it to come. Maybe I didn't want to be an unfeeling, jaded, robot member of the Unseen. Silence hung between us for the rest of the car ride, but my mind was less than silent. A little voice argued that Tracy wasn't that way. Sure, she seemed a little jaded, but she wasn't a robot, per se. She had feelings; I knew that better than anyone.

I sighed heavily and watched the changing landscape as we neared headquarters. The problem was that I wasn't Tracy, Owen, or Mitchell. And I didn't know how to deal with me.

We went straight to David's office as soon as we arrived. He was poring over some files on his desk when we came in.

"Please," he said, motioning toward the two chairs in front of his desk.

But I didn't want to sit. We'd been sitting for far too long, and Dr. Jeppe was close to something. I didn't fully understand what, but I knew it was terrible. That experiment with the monkeys had taken place almost a month ago. Who knew how much he progress he'd made since then. Maybe he'd successfully added the fourth chemical. Maybe not. It had seemed plenty deadly without it.

I paced back and forth while Tracy and David waited for me to start talking.

"Has she been like this the whole time?"

"Just since our last encounter with the scientist," Tracy said, not bothering to lower her voice for my sake. "She's been wildly emotional since then."

David nodded and went back to waiting.

"You were right," I said abruptly, deciding that was a good starting point. "He *is* evil." But I couldn't bring myself to continue quite yet. That would mean telling David about the experiments—saying those awful words out loud.

"How is he evil?" David asked. Both he and Tracy were watching me closely.

"His research..." I trailed off, searching for a way to make them understand without having to explain. I could have just shown them, of course—let them into my mind to see the horrifying vision. But no, I had to be stronger than that. This was my first assignment, and I had to do it justice. In the end, I swallowed the revulsion building in my stomach and told them everything. Right down to the screams. I flopped down heavily into the chair next to Tracy when I was finished.

"Who is Dux Ducis?" David asked.

"I don't know, some benefactor apparently. He approached Dr. Jeppe via email, and after that, they contacted each other solely via text messages. He's never heard his voice, let alone met him in person. I think he's a bit afraid of the guy, actually. And rightfully so, based on the threats he's been getting... not that he doesn't deserve them."

David frowned at that information. "Tracy, what do you think of his defenses?"

"I'm bothered by them, to be sure. From what Mackenzie said, it doesn't sound like he's a full-fledged member of the Potestas. I suspect someone in their ranks, possibly this Dux Ducis person, put the defenses in place in an attempt to protect the information in his mind."

"A disturbing proposition," David said.

"You can do that?" I'd never considered the defenses might have been set up by an outside party, but it made sense since there were no other indications Jeppe was a reader.

Tracy looked at me, a sly expression on her face. "You can do anything you put your mind to."

I rolled my eyes at her terrible pun. David smiled and said, "The important thing is to never assume something isn't possible. It can leave you open to attack. Tracy is right. In the world of the mind, anything is possible."

The conversation lulled for a moment, so I sat back in my chair, allowing my eyes to wander to David's desk. The file he'd been reading lay open on his desk, and there, plain as day, was Maddie's smiling face staring up at the ceiling.

The shock of seeing the image made me sit bolt upright in my chair and point accusingly at the file. The movement startled Tracy.

"Why do you have a picture of Maddie in that file?"

David sighed heavily. "I was just studying the incident, Mackenzie."

"David, I don't think this is a good time," Tracy said.

My world stopped. In that moment, the chimps were gone, and the scientist was no one. All I cared about was what was in that file. My hands started to shake, so I folded them in my lap in an attempt to show how mature and collected I was… not to mention totally prepared for whatever he had to say.

Clearing my throat, I said, "Now is as good a time as any."

David eyed me skeptically. "Tracy might be right. I wasn't anticipating the job to have such a deep impact on you. Perhaps we can discuss this later."

"No, please. I want to know."

Tracy frowned and leaned back in her chair, but then reconsidered and sat forward again. "David, I urge you not to discuss this matter at length right now. You weren't with her over the last twelve hours. She's been an emotional wreck. I don't even know what's in that file, but whatever it is could break her."

"You don't need to talk about me as if I'm not here." I took a deep breath. "And I can handle it. I know I can."

Tracy eyed me, but what she saw didn't change her mind any. "Mackenzie, this is not about some perceived weakness on your part. It's about your mental health. I've seen your mind. Your grief has made it terribly unstable. Whatever is in there, you may think you want to hear it, but I can assure you that you don't."

"How do you know?" I turned on her. "You never got any closer to finding your sister's killer, so you know how painful it is not to know who took her life. Why would you want to rob me of that knowledge?"

"What kind of closure do you think it will give you? Are you hoping that you'll find out Maddie's killers have already been eliminated? Is that what you want to see in that file? If so, you'll be disappointed. Usually, there's only vague, unconfirmed information about suspects. Do you want to live with that kind of frustration?" She paused for a moment, letting it sink in. "Or worse, what if it's evidence telling us the Potestas weren't involved at all? That Maddie, like everyone else on the train that day, was just a victim of a random act of violence, nothing more, nothing less. What will you do?"

"I don't know. But I should be given the chance to decide for myself."

David nodded. "The timing may be poor, but it's standard operating procedure for agents to get some time off after an assignment. You will have the rest of the day today and tomorrow free. Do with it what you will." He pushed the file toward me. "I will need that back in full when you're finished. You are not to make copies of it. I don't need sensitive information falling into the wrong hands." I nodded as I eyed the folder, not willing to touch it just yet.

"And I need you to be ready to go back to work Thursday. There's a lot to do." My eyes snapped up to him. The scientist. The chimps. The chemical. True, I didn't want people to die at the hands of Dux Ducis and the scientist, but my heart was in that folder. I could only hope I would have more focus once I had answers. Reaching forward, I took it off his desk and met Tracy's disapproving gaze head on.

"Thank you for this," I said to David, but I didn't break eye contact with Tracy.

"Are you sure you want to do this? The information in there…" He paused. "It won't be easy for you to read. If you want to talk about it, my door is open to you."

I nodded, but I wasn't sure I would feel much like talking… particularly not to him.

"Don't disappoint me, Mackenzie. We need you now, more than ever."

The statement stopped me short. "That's an odd choice of words," I said, even though I knew what he meant. But I'd heard that particular line so many times from my former aunt—*don't disappoint me, Mackenzie*—and I was through with being a disappointment to the people in my life. "Was it you who taught my 'aunt,'" I made quotation marks with my fingers, "to keep saying that to me while I was growing up without you?"

He stared at me slack-jawed as I walked out of his office, the file tucked carefully under my arm.

ELEVEN

Owen was waiting for me in the gym, but I walked right past him without really seeing him. I had tunnel vision. I planned to head straight for the work floor, pore over the file, find out who was responsible, and then...

And then what? The thought almost brought me to a stop right in the middle of the stairwell, and that was when Owen, who must have been trailing me for a while, alerted me to his presence.

"Hey!" He tugged on my arm. "I heard you were back, but by the time I got down here, you were already sequestered to David's office."

I looked down at his hand on me. "Hey." I blinked at him a few times, trying to bring myself back into the moment.

"How was the job?"

The job. The scientist. The chimps. The chemical. "You were right. David was right," I said, turning and continuing on my path upstairs.

Owen jogged to catch up to me. "Right about what?"

"That he was evil."

"Hey, can you stop for a second?" He was a little out of breath when he paused on the steps.

I turned to him, confused. He didn't understand. But then

again, how could he? He didn't know what was in the file under my arm. He probably thought it was about the scientist.

"This is the first I've seen you in two days. How about we start over?" He climbed the stairs slowly, holding his hands out toward me, acting like I was some skittish dog that was about to take off on him.

Realizing how tense my entire body was, I tried to force myself to relax.

He leaned in close and rested his forehead against mine. "Why don't we go somewhere quiet and talk about it?"

I shook my head. "No. There's more to do."

"It can wait. You have today and tomorrow off."

"No, I have today and tomorrow to work this out, then I have to start thinking about the scientist again."

Clearly, he was confused, and my cryptic answers weren't helping. Part of me really did want to stay right there in the stairwell, wrapped in his arms. Part of me wanted to let him offer me the comfort that my soul desperately needed. But the folder was heavy under my arm—it weighed on me, demanding answers, retribution.

Owen seemed to notice the file for the first time and pulled back. "Why do you still have that if you're off for the next day and a half? What is it?"

"Something that requires my attention." Why was I being so secretive? Did I think he'd try to talk me out of finding more about Maddie? Or was I just not prepared to take the time to explain it to someone? Either way, it didn't seem like a good way to treat someone you cared about. Guilt made me pause, and my mouth opened in preparation to tell him the truth. It was all there, ready to spill out. He might even help me read through the file. David's words came back to me. *The information in there won't be easy for you to read.* Did I want to be a total basket case in front of Owen... again? No.

Anyway, I reminded myself, this wasn't about Owen. It was about Maddie. I didn't even know what was in the folder. Once I did, I would be better equipped for his questions. At least, that was what I told myself as he stared at me with worried eyes.

"Right now?" His grip on my arm loosened a little, as if he already knew he'd lost this round.

I nodded, and he let me go completely.

"I'd like to spend some time with you. I missed you."

"Me too." I nodded quickly, hoping he heard my sincerity. But I wasn't ready to be what he wanted just yet. I needed to do this first. I needed to give this time to Maddie.

A sad expression passed over his face as he reached out and touched my arm lightly. "Come find me when you're done."

Again, I nodded and hesitated before I continued up the stairs on my own, leaving Owen alone in the stairwell. My heart wanted to be with him, to stay there, to accept his comfort. But what it wanted and what it needed were two different things.

I didn't pay attention to my surroundings as I rushed down the hallway of the correct floor, looking for an empty workroom, so it surprised me when Mitchell rather abruptly stepped out of the room I was walking past.

I nodded a greeting at him, but he didn't nod back. He pulled the door closed behind him and stepped in front of me, coming to a careful stop.

Eyeing the folder in my arms, he sighed. "Just be careful. Use your head, okay? Not your heart."

"I don't know what you're talking about." It wasn't a lie. How could he possibly know what I was up to? Maybe he was talking about the work I'd done on the scientist? Either way, I wasn't interested in wasting brainpower on it at the moment. I had bigger fish to fry.

"Right," he said, his tone skeptical, almost suspicious. I shrugged him off and sequestered myself in an empty workroom.

Leaning back in the chair, I let exhaustion take me for a moment. It was only about four o'clock, but it felt like midnight after everything I'd been through. Frankly, I was worried Tracy was right, that I wasn't entirely prepared for whatever the file contained. I might finally be holding the key to Maddie's death. All I had to do was read.

I glanced at the file in front of me, feeling like Pandora must have as she sat before a certain box. Once I read the contents, I couldn't unread them, I couldn't unlearn whatever horrors lay waiting for me inside. Or maybe there was nothing inside. Maybe the file simply contained empty lead after empty lead, with no real answers. Or maybe her death truly had been a senseless accident. What would I do then?

The questions kept coming, so I silenced them by throwing the file open.

Maddison Farland
Born: July 2, 1989
Died: September 21, 2014
Cause of death: Terrorist attack
Suspects involved: Aydin Nascimbeni, Washington Lange, Curtis Kingsley

Headshots of all three men had been clipped right behind Maddie's. Staring at their faces, I supposed the word "men" was a bit generous. They were probably not much older than I was. In fact, they were each kind of attractive in their own way. Under different circumstances, I might have flirted with boys like them. How had they become killers?

I read on, noticing a hastily scrawled note near the list of suspects.

Amanda?

I read the name again. It couldn't be her, could it? According to David, she'd disappeared and no one had heard from her since my graduation. The woman I'd known as my aunt couldn't have been involved in Maddie's death...

David's voice echoed in my head: *Never assume something isn't possible.* Did she hate me that much? Of course she did. I'd listened to her thoughts all day, every day, for years. But Maddie? How could she do something so horrible to someone like Maddie? She was always kind to my aunt; she'd even gone so far as to make gifts for her on Christmas and her birthday. She was always the first person to remind me to give my "aunt" the benefit of the doubt. I had wanted to believe her, of course, but I'd always known the truth. It was hard to ignore.

Now, even more of that awful truth was staring back at me in messy handwriting, refusing to be disputed. But what role could she have played, really? Had she turned coat and led them right to her? Why her? Why not me?

The file held no answers, so I spent the rest of the day searching the Internet and the Unseen's databases for the names in Maddie's file, starting with my "aunt."

Amanda Day was a bit of a ghost, at least to me. Apparently, I didn't know her real last name, because I found no relevant search results. At times, it had bugged her that we shared the same last name, as she didn't care to be mistaken for my mother. According to the story she'd told me, she was my dad's never-married sister. Her perpetual singleness had confused me when I was younger, but I ultimately decided it made all the sense in the world that no one would want to spend their life with such a negative person. I searched the website of her old employer and found nothing. In fact, I couldn't even find any record of the accounting firm where she supposedly worked. I knew it existed. I'd been there more than once. How had it just disappeared into thin air? If they'd gone out of business, wouldn't there be some kind of paper trail? Making a mental note to ask David what he knew about my aunt, I moved on. I made a separate mental note to stop calling her my aunt.

Surprisingly, I found a fair bit of information on the boys. Oddly, the three weren't geographically close to each other. The one named Aydin lived in Texas, Curtis lived in Illinois, but Washington lived right here in Tallahassee. What were the odds of that? Did he have some connection to me? I stared at his high school picture on the computer screen. He was dark and handsome, and his expression was intensely sultry, as if he'd known women would be looking at the picture.

Finding his address was a simple matter, and despite the fact that it might interfere with the Unseen's investigation, I knew

I had to see him for myself. A glance at my watch told me I'd missed dinner. I leaned back in the chair and rubbed my eyes, groaning.

If the boys were so easy to find, why couldn't I find anything about Amanda? I wondered what David knew about the investigation of Washington and the other guys. Maybe he could even tell me something about Amanda. Despite our recently tense exchanges, my drive to know more about what happened to Maddie outweighed my pride.

My body cringed when I stood up, complaining after so much sitting. Stretching, I tried to appease my sore muscles and made my way back downstairs.

Mitchell was working out in the gym when I got there, and I groaned at the sight of him. Despite the fact that he wasn't the lecturing type, I knew he disapproved of whatever he thought I was doing. I had no idea why, and at that moment, I didn't really care.

Thankfully, he could tell where I was headed based on the angle I took across the gym. He simply nodded at me. I returned the gesture and knocked on David's door.

It was almost seven, so I didn't really expect him to still be around. He didn't sleep at the facility with the rest of us. In fact, I wasn't sure where he went after "work." He never hung around and watched movies with the rest of the Unseen, and he never ate meals with us. I figured it was some boss/employee hierarchy thing. He probably just wanted to let the peons have their time together. Don't make things awkward by having the friendly boss swoop in. Anyway, I could only hope he was still there. I didn't want to wait until morning to get my questions answered. I had other plans for my day.

To my surprise, he responded to my knock. "Come in."

"I didn't think you'd still be here."

"Someone brought some alarming new information to my attention today. It required further scrutiny."

I wrinkled my chin and sat down across from him. "Hey David, where do you go when you're not here? If it's a rule for us to live here, why don't you?"

"What makes you think I don't live here?"

"Because I never see you milling around the facility. You don't have a room on our floor. And I never see you in the bathroom. Those are all pretty good indications that you don't stay here."

He smiled. "All valid points. But I'd rather not say, especially to you. As my daughter, you're a highly valued target. The less you know, the better."

"In your worst-case scenario, they're going to think I know all this anyway. They'll torture me to death trying to get the information whether I know it or not."

He frowned. "Maybe."

"Don't you think being your daughter should come with some perks instead of so many restrictions?"

A small smile lifted one corner of his mouth. "The office is the entryway to my suite. There's a hidden panel that opens to my apartment, equipped with my own kitchen, bathroom, living room, and bedroom. I live here too, just like the rest of you."

"Huh. I'd like to see it sometime," I said, trying to picture how far back it went.

"Let's not get carried away. Is that why you came down here? To ask me where I sleep?"

Though I was suddenly curious about whether there were other secret compartments inside the facility, I forced myself to return to the problems at hand. "I want to know about Amanda."

"You read the file then?" I put it on the desk, and he reached out for it. "Thank you."

"Thank you for showing it to me. Now, tell me what you know about her."

"Oddly, nothing. She really has disappeared. My moles tell me she's joined the other side, which would make sense given the way her entire existence has been erased."

"It doesn't make sense to me. The other three in that file were super easy to find. If she were a traitor, wouldn't she be less protected than them rather than more?"

"Not necessarily. And her level of anonymity tells me she's

stepped into a fairly high position. Of course, this is all just speculation. I can't set too much stock in the information the moles give to us. They tell me what the Potestas want me to know."

"Why would she do such a thing?" I hadn't thought she still possessed the power to hurt me, but if even a small part of what David had said was true, I was horribly wrong. She'd betrayed me in every way possible.

"I think she did it to get back at me for making her…" he hesitated, but said the word anyway, "babysit you for so long."

"You think this is about you?" It surprised me, as I'd never considered the possibility. Based on what I knew, on what I'd heard from her thoughts, she hated *me*. I'd never heard a single thought about him. Although, now that I thought about it, that had been probably been a calculated move on her part.

"Of course it is. What did you think?"

"That she hated me so much that she has a vendetta against me."

He actually laughed out loud. "It's also possible she doesn't have a vendetta against either of us. Perhaps she just found herself a very nice position with our competitor, and she's in a good place to elevate herself further by exploiting us. Or, before we're too hasty, it's possible the Potestas have gotten ahold of her and killed her, erasing all traces of her existence."

I cringed at the thought. She was nothing if not selfish. But I didn't really want her dead. "It isn't good, no matter how you slice it."

"No, it isn't."

Silence settled over the room as we each retreated to our own thoughts. Eventually, David spoke up. "All three of the suspects are being monitored closely, as we try to find connections between them, the SunRail, and the Potestas." He paused, watching me carefully. "Tell me something. The boy, Washington, what are your intentions with him?"

"I'm already dating someone, Daddy." I'd meant it to sound tongue in cheek. The way he'd phrased the question was so fatherly. But the d-word hung in the air between us, changing the atmosphere in the room.

He let it go and smiled just a little. "You know what I mean."

Rather than flat-out lie to him, I put off responding.

He sighed. "Please, Mackenzie. Don't make me regret giving you the file."

The exhaustion in his voice almost made my resolve waiver.

"I don't know what you're talking about. I plan to spend the day shopping for a new dress for Coda."

David eyed me. "I want to believe that."

"You should. It's the truth." So much for not lying to him. But it was a brilliant cover, and I mentally patted myself on the back, even if it was a horribly deceitful thing to do.

"Okay, well, enjoy yourself then. I'll see you at eight sharp on Thursday morning. There's much to discuss."

Taking that as my dismissal, I rose. "Okay." I left his office feeling just as confused as I'd felt going in, except for different reasons.

Thankfully, Mitchell was gone by the time I left, and a glance at my watch told me I'd been in there for less than an hour. Owen would probably be upstairs watching a movie. I felt I should do the courteous thing and at least say hello to him, but I found myself dreading it. All I wanted to do was go to bed. Too many things were at war in my mind. Amanda, Maddie, Washington, Jeppe, the chemical, Owen, Mitchell. Which one was most important? Which one deserved the bulk of my attention?

I shook my head and made my way up to the living room, trying to prepare myself for Owen's third degree.

As expected, I found Owen draped lazily on the couch near Mitchell. He got up and came over as soon as he spotted me.

"I wasn't sure I'd see you again today," he said, his voice pitched low so he didn't disturb the movie watchers.

"I just wanted to say goodnight. I'm toast."

"Mitchell said you went to see David again."

"I did." I glanced at our friend, who didn't bother averting his eyes. I couldn't be upset with him. It wasn't a secret. And he obviously wasn't sorry for telling on me.

"Did you work everything out? Will you be off tomorrow so we can spend some time together?"

That thought hadn't even occurred to me. I groaned, knowing he wouldn't be happy with my cover story. But something deep inside me was driving me to seek closure over Maddie's death, something that went even deeper than my feelings for Owen.

"I do have tomorrow off, but I want to find a dress for Coda."

His face fell, and I knew I'd hurt him. He was the one person who'd steadily been there for me through everything, which made disappointing him that much worse.

He tried to smile. "Oh. Don't you think that could wait a little while? I really want to spend some time with you."

"No. They need me back at work on Thursday. This job is bigger than any of us thought it would be, so I don't know when I'll get another opportunity. I want to be ready for our big date." I smiled, hoping it would be enough.

"I'm sure you'll find something great." He leaned in and planted a light kiss on my lips, then turned to walk away, trying to hide his disappointment. I grabbed his arm, not wanting to part from him on such terms, even for a few hours.

"Owen, I'm sorry. But I wanted to have at least one new dress for this event. I thought you wanted me to be excited about it. I'll try to be back after lunch and we can spend the rest of the day together. Okay?" I hoped that would give me enough time to accomplish my undefined goals for the following day.

He perked up a little, but still pouted, probably to get more sympathy out of me. "All right, I guess. And I *am* glad you're excited about Coda. I hear it's kind of a big deal."

I chuckled and shook my head. "Now, take your sad puppy expression and go back to your movie. I'm going to bed."

"Already?"

"Job? Travel? Exhaustion? Any of this ringing a bell?"

"Oh. Right. Well, have fun tomorrow. I'll see you after lunch." He leaned forward and kissed me. The softness of it let me know he forgave me. I trudged back downstairs and gratefully crawled into my bed, trying to put his sad puppy face out of my head.

Owen was a trouble for another day. Tomorrow, I would face a killer.

TWELVE

I t was early when I pulled up in front of the guy's apartment. I was hoping to catch him before he left for work. Cursing myself for not having looked up where he worked, I stewed in the parking lot for at least an hour. There was no sight of him. Maybe he was off that day? It was possible I'd already missed him, but when I glanced at my watch, I saw it was only 8:07 am. I didn't think it was likely he'd left yet unless he worked some seven to seven shift. In which case, I was totally screwed.

I just planned to talk to him. I hadn't decided if I would call him out or not. The most important thing was to gather information. According to David, the Unseen were watching him closely already, and I didn't want to interfere... too much. I just wanted to hear for myself if he was responsible. That was all. I hoped it would give me closure, I guess.

Suddenly, he emerged from the building. Dressed in jeans and a brown suede jacket with the collar turned up, he turned and walked east down the sidewalk, his back to me. I scrambled out of the car, almost falling in my haste, and jogged to catch up with him.

Slowing my pace behind him, I allowed some carefully curated thoughts to escape in the hopes of catching his attention.

He's so cute. I wonder if he has a girlfriend waiting for him. I bet he keeps her warm on these cold nights.

I had just enough time to wipe the smirk from my face before he turned around. "So, you think I'm cute, huh?"

I feigned surprise. "I didn't say that."

"You didn't have to." He moved in close to me, and I looked up at him. His dark hair was cropped short and gelled to stand straight up, and his chocolate eyes were rimmed with criminally long eyelashes. No guy should have lashes that dark and thick. He scrutinized my face from behind them.

"Call it an instinct."

Playing coy, I smiled and looked away.

"Why don't we go someplace a little quieter where we can…" He paused. "Get to know each other."

His smooth moves and confidence made it hard to push down the bile that had climbed into my throat.

Hooking my arm in his, I let him lead me away. It was a nice day outside, if not a little cool. The sun was shining, and a light breeze kept the air around us fresh. It was the perfect day for a walk with an enemy.

I knew the neighborhood fairly well, as it turned out we weren't all that far from my old apartment. A few turns and street crosses later, we found ourselves in a quiet little café.

"Huh, this place is pretty empty."

"Just how I like it."

"I bet it's not how the owner likes it," I said. A crowd would have suited me better as well, but I could hardly say that to him.

After we ordered and retrieved our coffees at the counter, we sat across from each other at one of the small, round tables. The rest were empty. "You're a bit puzzling," he said, his gaze narrowing on me.

"Why?"

"Most women are full of emotions and questions, not to mention thoughts and opinions about all kinds of things. But you seem very quiet."

A normal person might have assumed he was calling me an introvert, but I didn't miss the deeper meaning. I wasn't letting my thoughts leak through like a normal person would. Panic started to settle in as I tried to take control. If I overdid it now, he'd be suspicious. If he discovered my defenses, I'd be toast.

"I like to practice yoga. It keeps my mind clear."

He eyed me, clearly still suspicious, and panic thrummed through me. What would he do if he recognized me? After all, the people who killed Maddie did it to get to me. Wouldn't they have pictures on file, or did David do that good of a job at hiding me?

Desperate, I tried to divert him. "So, what's a good-looking guy like you doing spontaneously taking a girl out for coffee? Surely you must have obligations. A girlfriend?" I added with a coy quality to my voice, hoping he was the type of guy who was controlled by his ego.

His smile stretched from ear to ear, and I let out a breath, knowing I'd won this round. "No, I don't date steadily. I prefer to keep things light—flirt a little, have some fun."

I chuckled to cover up a snort of derision. "And that works?"

"Worked on you."

"Besides me."

"Worked great on this girl on the train a few weeks back. She practically threw herself at me."

I gritted my teeth. "I'm not sure I want all the gritty details of your last conquest." It was a lie. Of course I wanted to know, it was why I was there, but a casual date wouldn't react with curiosity.

"She wasn't exactly a conquest. More of an assignment."

Knowing all too well what that meant, I asked. "Oh? What happened to her?"

"She... our relationship met with an untimely end." He never missed a beat. There was a smug smile on his face, like he was actually proud of what he'd done to her. As he took a sip of his mocha-caramel-frappe confection, I realized I hadn't even touched mine.

"From the look on your face, I'd say you were glad to be rid of her." It came out through my teeth, and I hoped he didn't notice the strain. Anger heated my insides—sudden, intense, and agonizing. The arrogance, the conversation, the hungry way he looked at me, it was all too much.

"Let's just say, getting rid of her did good things for my career." He paused, looking kind of wistful. "I might even be able to quit my day job soon."

That was all it took. The rage boiled over inside me, and without thinking, I took control of the situation—and him. We sat for a moment in what he probably thought was companionable silence, when in reality I was making my way past his weak defenses. Soon, I found myself deep inside his fragile mind.

Sipping my coffee, I watched his memories whizz by. I purposely didn't focus on the SunRail explosion. I didn't need or want to watch it. As it turned out, Maddie hadn't been his only victim. Most were men, but he'd killed women too… even a child. What kind of threat could a child have possibly posed? I counted almost a dozen deaths at his hand, and none of the murders had made him feel the smallest amount of guilt. I didn't even know how to process the information. The visions haunted me, until I could take no more.

"Well, I think our time together is up," I said, standing up and walking away from the table, knowing he would follow me, willingly or not. We walked a few streets over before coming to a street busy enough to suit my purposes. On the walk, my resolve wavered a bit, but then I remembered how he'd smiled after saying Maddie's death had done good things for his career. And I could never forget the face of the child whose life he had snuffed out. No, I could not let this man get away. I just couldn't.

I increased my pace, and he tagged along behind me like some puppy.

Once we were in a busy enough spot, I turned to face him. "Do you know who I am?" Confusion played on his face. "Did you even know who Maddie was, or why you were told to kill her?"

His eyes narrowed, and I could see the struggle on his face, but it was for nothing. I had complete control of him, and he was starting to understand that.

Taking a step toward him, I draped my arms around his neck. To any passersby, we would've looked like a normal couple, except I made sure to keep his hands by his sides. I didn't want him touching me ever again.

"I am Mackenzie Day. A name you'll never forget." I leaned in and kissed him on the cheek for effect. And then I turned him around without touching him, and walked him directly into the street.

I'd never been inside a mind as it died before. It was a rather shocking and unpleasant experience, to be honest. The Greyhound bus barreled down on him, with no hope of stopping. The horn blared, and Washington turned to face it, his horror written on his face. He wanted to lift his arms, to shield himself from it, but I wouldn't let him do even that. I wanted him to take the full force of the bus. I wanted him to watch it barrel down on him without being able to stop it or even jump out of its way. A scream bubbled in his mind, but I didn't allow it to surface. To an onlooker, he would seem very purposeful. Suicidal. I smiled at the horror I felt in his mind.

Now you know how Maddie felt, I told him as the bus careened toward him, squealing its tires and blaring its horn.

He tried to look at me, but I kept him staring straight at the bus. *No. You stupid bitch, you'll pay for this. No!*

The bus came to a screeching halt at least four car lengths from the point of impact. The pain I felt in that moment was excruciating, and I nearly tumbled to the ground.

In the aftermath of the accident, there were cries of shock, pointing fingers, and several people pulling out their phones for 911 calls. I just stood and stared at the back of the bus, feeling nothing. Maybe I was in shock.

Eventually, the pain faded, and I knew he was dead.

In the chaos, I noticed a man on the other side of the street, staring directly at me. But before I could get a good look, Owen was beside me, urging me to leave.

"Come on, Mackenzie," he said, pulling me along by the elbow.

"What are you doing here?"

"Perhaps a better question is what are *you* doing here?" He glanced over his shoulder at the place where the man had been.

It was empty. "You know what? It doesn't matter right now. Let's go."

Feeling drained suddenly, I relented and let him lead me on a rather winding route back to his car. "Seems like that was the long way around," I said as he threw me into the passenger's seat.

Instead of addressing my statement, he asked, "Where did you leave the Unseen's car?"

I gave him the address and he raced to it, driving rather recklessly around the city streets. "We have to get it before they start investigating."

"What's the big deal? To all the witnesses, it looked like he just walked out into the street."

"But all the witnesses saw you hanging on to him and whispering to him before he did it. They also took in the fact that you didn't react at all." His hands tightened on the steering wheel.

"That doesn't mean anything. People deal with shock in all different ways. Don't you want to know who he was? Owen, he was a murderer. He'd killed a lot of people."

"I don't care who he was, Mackenzie. I care who you are. Frankly, I'm not sure I like that girl right now."

Feeling at once deflated, confused by what I'd just done, and still angry, I couldn't comprehend what he was saying to me. Wasn't this what the Unseen did?

Folding my arms over my chest like a defeated child, I said, "Well, fine." It came out more indignant than I'd intended. "What were you doing there anyway?" I asked.

"David asked me to follow you today. He thought you were up to something. I wanted to prove him wrong. Apparently, he won that bet."

"He had me followed?" I tried to feel violated, but he was right. I certainly had been up to something, even though I'd had no idea how far it would go.

After a few moments of silence, we arrived at Washington's apartment. Before I could get out of the car, Owen spoke again.

"You were seen."

"I know I was seen. There were a ton of people milling

around."

"No, you were seen by the Potestas."

THIRTEEN

I didn't know what to do with that information, so I said nothing and got out of the car, gratefully taking in the silence and emptiness of my own car. Following Owen back to the facility proved difficult given the way he was driving, but we made it back in record time.

After parking the car in the Unseen's underground parking garage, I sat there for a moment quietly, thinking about the man on the other side of the road. It must've been him. He was the only one who'd seemed out of place. But I'd only seen him for an instant, and I couldn't remember any of his features. There was no way I'd be able to pick him out of a lineup.

Before I was ready, Owen ended my meditation and hauled me out of the car by the arm.

I spotted Mitchell on our way down to David's office, but he didn't say anything. Just looked at me. There was no judgment in his eyes, but no approval either.

Owen slammed me into the chair across from David's desk. Tracy was already there, mid-conversation with David. Both of them were visibly upset.

"The witnesses are being handled, and I don't mind telling you, there were a lot of them," she said.

"Sorry to interrupt," I said, rotating my shoulder and trying to work out the ache Owen had left there after jerking me down four flights of stairs.

"Actually, we're talking about you," David said.

Owen interjected before he could continue. He paced the small office rapidly, making me dizzy. "You said you weren't a murderer. You dumped me for being one, even though I've never killed someone like that—someone who wasn't actually a direct threat to me or thousands of other people." He pointed his finger accusingly at me, but the guilt I should've felt eluded me.

"He was a direct threat."

"To who?" David asked.

"He'd killed people other than Maddie. Lots of people. And a—" I choked on the word, but then cleared my throat and got it out. It had to be said. They had to understand. "A kid. He killed a little kid."

They were quiet for a bit. "He didn't even know who Maddie was," I said, the words coming out of my mouth as if on their own accord. "It was just a job for him. He didn't seem to know who I was either."

"They do now!" Owen yelled. "I bet all the Potestas have a pretty little picture of your sick grin as you walked that guy in front of a bus. You were being watched the whole freaking time!"

David held up his hand, and Owen quieted down. I didn't realize how loud he'd been talking until he stopped. My ears rang a little as David started in on me. "How could you be so reckless?" His tone was low, accusing, and dangerous.

But I wasn't threatened. I was vindicated, so I held my chin up in response. I'd done the right thing. I'd killed a remorseless killer. Until the moment it happened, I hadn't even known I was capable of such a thing.

He frowned as he went on. "As members of the Unseen, we must operate with the highest level of discretion. What you did is the complete opposite of that. Had it been a mission, there would have been sweeps of the area to make sure it was free of Potestas. You would've been covered. But this…" He trailed off. "This is a mess."

"And the clean-up procedure will be extensive because of the way you handled it," Tracy added. "Not to mention the fact that the other suspects in Maddie's murder are lost causes. The Potestas will know you're targeting them, and by now, their identities will have been wiped clean."

Okay. I hadn't achieved the perfect execution. But I'd still done the right thing. Right?

Before my resolve could waver, I spoke up. "He deserved it."

David thrust a file at me. It was Washington's. "You know, if you'd given this to me earlier, it would've saved me a lot of work." I was trying to be funny, but no one laughed.

I flipped it open and started looking through papers. Some of it I already knew—his name, age, address, things like that. But there was new information too. Apparently his "day job," as he'd put it, was working at Foot Locker as an assistant manager. He also had a younger sister who would be graduating from FSU in two years, and two parents who seemed to dote on them both. I frowned at their latest family portrait. If David was trying to elicit some kind of sympathetic response because the killer had a family, he'd missed his mark.

"What kind of people could raise such a monster?" Shoving the file back to David, I sat back in the chair, trying to contain my revulsion.

"The kind of people who've just had their son taken from them, the kind of people who will have a hard time swallowing the fact that he was suicidal and walked out in front of that bus on purpose. That's what all the witnesses are saying."

"And the people who had their toddler taken from them? Maddie's family? What about them?"

"Clearly, I'm not getting through to you," David said, his frustration evident.

I sighed, feeling tired and sad. "David, I didn't intend to kill him. I went to his house because I didn't think I'd ever be at peace if I didn't confront him. One thing led to another, and I couldn't stop myself from reading him. Once I saw what was in his mind... I *couldn't* let him go, I just couldn't. He had no regrets, so why should I?"

Owen couldn't hold on to his tongue anymore. "This is exactly what we were all worried you would do. And you proved us right." His eyes narrowed. "The worst part is that you aren't even sorry." He shook his head and stormed out of the office.

Tracy chuckled shortly.

"What's so funny?"

"You. Not that long ago, you were obsessively in love with him. I've never seen him so angry, so he's clearly in love with you. A few weeks ago, that little tantrum would've had you groveling at his feet. But you're just sitting there, your chin held high." She shook her head. "Now, I don't support groveling of any kind, but the fact that you're so staunchly standing behind what you did is bothersome, Mackenzie.

"If nothing else, you have made this world much more dangerous for yourself. You had some anonymity before. You obliterated that with your act of revenge. Don't you care about your own safety?"

"Apparently not." I agreed with her assertion more than I wanted to. She'd made a good point.

David threw up his hands and threw himself back in his chair. Looking at Tracy, he said, "I don't even know how to deal with this." He jabbed a finger at me, and then continued. "How about this? What you've done is completely against company policy. You've exterminated a human being."

"A member of the Potestas. The enemy, as you yourself have called them. An enemy who killed at least a dozen people."

David frowned. "Yes. You've found a nice little gray area for yourself, haven't you? If you think you're going to go unpunished for what you've done, you can think again."

"I never expected to go unpunished, David." I put special emphasis on his name. I couldn't call him Dad. Not now. Maybe not ever, after what I'd done. "I just wanted to get justice for Maddie and the others."

"And is that really what Maddie would've wanted?" Tracy's tone was quiet. The statement cut through me like a sword through a piece of paper, but she kept on. "You always said what a great person she was, so happy and bubbly all the time. Would she have wanted such an ugly vengeance?"

No. Maddie's voice echoed in the back of my mind. *No.* My eyes pleaded with them as I looked from Tracy to David. *No.* An eye for an eye, right? *No.* The word pulsed in my brain until I put my hands over my ears and shut my eyes. Pulling my knees up to my face, I created my own personal cocoon in the chair. But Maddie kept talking.

I want you to be happy, she said. *That's all I want.*

Soon, I felt Tracy's hands on my shoulders. I risked opening my eyes a little, and found her mere inches from my face. "Unfortunately, we don't have time for a breakdown right now." I should've known she wasn't going to be sympathetic.

I looked at David, hoping for support, something, but his expression hadn't budged.

Feeling alone and unwanted, I looked into David's disapproving face. Somehow, I still couldn't bring myself to say I was sorry. I didn't regret taking that man's life, but it was hard to forgive myself for dishonoring Maddie and endangering the others.

"Tracy is right. There's work to do. Today, you will be confined to isolation. Your privileges are being revoked. Tomorrow, you will go back to work. And I mean *work.* None of this vigilante crap. I need you focused and on top of your game. This is serious, Mackenzie. People's lives are at stake. A lot of people's lives. We all believe you can save them, if you can manage to pull it together… if you can manage to put other people above your own personal agenda."

I had no defense for that, so I let Tracy escort me to the locked room at the very back of the work floor, the one with the cot, sink, and toilet. I was right—it *was* for prisoners. The front of the cell was equipped with a floor-to-ceiling window that would allow around-the-clock supervision of the prisoner inside—in this case, me. The speaker near the door ensured I could speak with visitors, not that I expected any.

Tracy said nothing as she locked me into the cell. She didn't have to. The disappointment was plain in her drawn expression, her stiff posture, and the way she looked at me. She'd expected more from me. But I wasn't sure what. I'd done extraordinary things. Just because I hadn't done them exactly how they wanted me to...

No. That was a vindictive and self-destructive path to follow. I'd done wrong by Maddie. That was what mattered. Problem was, I had no idea how to make it right. Maddie was dead. It wasn't like I could apologize to her.

Left alone in the cell, the events of the day finally started to penetrate my state of shock. A man died at my hands, rather horribly.

I lay down on the cot and turned my back to the outside world. Even in death, Maddie was a better friend than I was. Now, I could do nothing but live with that fact.

"Turns out, neither one of us was right, Maddie," I said to the wall through my tears. "I'm not a savior. I'm nothing but a killer."

Sometime in the night, I drifted off. It was Mitchell who woke me up with a light knock on the window. He was sitting in a chair he must have dragged from one of the workrooms.

"I was hoping Owen would come by," I said, wiping my eyes, willing them to focus after so little sleep.

"He's pretty pissed at you."

I nodded, not needing to hear more. We sat in silence for a few moments, like we so often did. Except this time, I could feel something hanging in the air, like a strange sort of pressure.

Eager to relieve it, I prompted him. "Why'd you come here, Mitchell?"

He didn't look at me. Instead, he just kept staring down the long, quiet hallway. I knew him well enough to realize he was deep in thought.

"I didn't even see them coming." It came out quietly. So quietly in fact, I almost didn't hear him. I sat up and scooted to the edge of the bed, as if getting closer would help.

"They wrecked *me*. Not anyone else. I didn't have anyone else for them to wreck. I was already an orphan by then, through no fault of theirs." He glanced at me and shrugged.

I'd never heard Mitchell's story, and had no idea what was prompting him to tell it to me now, but I silently urged him to go on, completely enraptured with his tale.

"But what they did to me… I can't explain it. They thought I was dead. But I wasn't. Somehow, by some miracle—or maybe some cosmic joke—I was left alive."

"They hacked into my mind, tortured me in ways I've never been able to tell anyone. Not even David. And then…" He trailed off, his expression distant.

Getting up off the bed, I crossed the room, if for no other reason than to be closer to him. I put my hand against the window right next to him. But he didn't see. He was in another world, watching his memories.

He blinked and took a deep breath. When he turned to look through the window at me, he didn't seem startled by my sudden closeness. He simply went on with his story. "At any rate, they made it very difficult for me to differentiate between the world they'd created and reality. Even after David and his people rescued me. I couldn't enjoy an ice cream sundae without suspecting it wasn't real."

"An ice cream sundae?"

"Yeah." He glanced over at me and shrugged. "They're my favorite. And the Potestas knew it. They liked to exploit that fact. Frequently."

Slowly, I sat back, still keeping my hand on the glass, trying to make a connection with the broken person on the other side.

"What they did to me made me so angry. They destroyed the person I was."

My head snapped up. He was angry too? Everyone always acted like I was the only person in the history of the Unseen to react that way.

"In fact, I was so angry that I went back to the place where they'd tortured me. Years had passed, but I still remembered it like I'd lived there my whole life. Small details stood out to me, like the single, bare lightbulb that hung in the room where they'd tried to break me."

Silence hung between us for a few beats, so I decided to risk a question. "Mitchell, why? Why did they do that to you?"

"You know, at the time, I didn't understand. I was an orphan who could read minds. I wasn't really anything special. My foster families could vouch for that."

His frankness pulled at my heartstrings. He'd been through so much, yet he was still somehow holding it together. I, on the other hand, was a complete and total wreck.

"When I went back, I asked that very question to the man I found there. At first, he didn't even remember me. But, after some persuasion, his memory came back. He said they wanted to get to me before the Unseen did. That's all it was. I asked him why they didn't recruit me instead. Apparently, they needed talented subjects for their trainees. For them, I was nothing more than a target for shooting practice."

"It was slow and messy. But I didn't kill him." He looked at me then, a sad smile on his face. "I did him one worse than you. I destroyed his mind, leaving him a drooling vegetable. When I walked away, he was nothing but a worthless shell of a body."

Were he and I really so similar? If so, maybe he could help me find a way out. "Mitchell," I said quietly. "How did you come back from such a dark place?"

"I didn't. At least, not right away. I was pleased with what I'd done. Owen wasn't sure how to handle me at first. He couldn't understand why I would destroy someone like that. Despite what you thought of him at first, he's pretty black and white when it comes to killing people. But, he's still a good friend and a brother in arms, so he tried to be supportive while constantly telling me what I'd done was wrong.

"I didn't agree for a long time. Years. Only when I managed to let go of my anger did I see the violation I'd made. I hadn't just killed someone—I'd ruined their life."

"But—" I started, not sure how I would've finished if Mitchell hadn't interrupted me.

"But nothing. That was the fact of the matter. Every once in a while, I check on him. He's in an assisted living facility, eating from a tube because his family can't bear to let him go. One time, I even stopped in to see him. To tell him I was sorry. But

I couldn't do it. The silence coming from the other side of the door was crushing. I'd left nothing untouched, and it showed."

He sighed, the weight of what he'd done evidenced by his hunched shoulders. "In the end, I knew it wouldn't do me any good. So I left. I haven't been back since. That was right before you joined us."

I scooted back and leaned against the wall, looking in the same direction as Mitchell. Resting my arms on my knees, I looked down the hallway, hoping to reconcile what I'd just learned with my own future.

What kinds of people use an ice cream sundae against you as torture? These are the people who deserve mercy? I thought. But justification wasn't the right path to follow, and I knew it.

"Boy, I could sure go for an ice cream sundae right about now," I said, trying to distract myself from the tension around me.

He laughed. "When you get out, I'll show you what a real sundae is. Homemade caramel sauce like you'll never get out of a jar." His smile lit up his face. It gave me hope to think he could still enjoy a thing that had been so terribly used against him.

"It's a date," I said. "Hey, Mitch, can I ask you something?" He nodded, so I went on. "How did you know what I was going to do?" He didn't answer, so I prodded him a little more. "After I got back from my first job, I was carrying Maddie's folder, not the scientist's, when I came up here to work. You stopped me in the hall and told me to use caution. How did you know?"

He sighed and scrubbed his face with both hands. Finally, he said, "I've been trying to find your… aunt. David is concerned about that particular loose end. I knew David was planning to share the intel we had on Maddie with you, and when I saw you come back from your job with another file, I put two and two together."

I leaned my head back against the wall. *David was working to find answers, if not for Maddie, then for my safety.* I'd really blown it.

Mitchell added one more thing before he left me with my thoughts. "I didn't tell you any of this to make you feel sorry for me, or to tell you you're not alone or some other BS. I told you so you'd know what the world is like on the other side of this glass. It's different, now that you've killed someone on purpose. But that doesn't make life unlivable."

"But… Maddie." My voice cracked, made unstable by sorrow.

"But nothing. Maddie is dead. If she were still alive, she'd have every right to judge you for what you'd done. But things being what they are, I don't think she much cares either way. Let it go."

I cringed at his harsh words, but he didn't see. He was already walking down the long hallway, leaving me alone to consider the road I'd already walked, and the one that lay before me.

Two paths diverged in a yellow wood. Maddie's voice echoed in my mind. It seemed ages ago when she'd said that to me. My choices had seemed so much simpler then—one job over another, not one life over another.

"Well," I said aloud to the room, hoping she'd hear me. "I certainly took the road less traveled."

In the following silence, I decided to try to get some rest. I didn't know what the road ahead held for me, but whatever it was, I wanted to be ready.

FOURTEEN

Tracy came to get me in what I assumed was the morning. Without windows or any natural source of light, the Unseen relied on their watches and clocks to separate day from night. I didn't have my watch, and there was no clock in the cell, so I was sleeping when Tracy showed up. She seemed only slightly irritated at having to wait.

Surprisingly, I'd slept rather well in the cell. I suspected my exhaustion had finally caught up with me and silenced my concerns about my future.

It only took me a few moments to haul myself out of bed and get ready to go with her. I didn't intend to push her patience by dilly-dallying. She walked me down to David's office in companionable silence. I really didn't have anything to say to her right then. Either she understood, or she didn't. Nothing I could say would change that. I had no idea if what I'd done would change our relationship. I hoped not, but I didn't have any control over it, and somehow, I'd come to peace with that.

What Mitchell told me the night before had hit home, and I hoped I could take the same peaceful approach with Owen. If he came around and decided he still wanted me in his life, I'd be there in a minute. If not, hopefully I could let him go. The thought made me catch my breath, but I pushed forward as we entered David's office to receive our assignments.

It surprised me to see Owen sitting in the chair Tracy usually occupied. He stood when Tracy came in, offering it to her, but she grabbed another one from one of the training rooms.

Once we were crowded around his desk, David didn't waste any time getting started. "Mackenzie." His sharp tone startled me, forcing me to look straight at him. "I realize it might be a mistake to trust you with the upcoming job, but we don't have anyone else with the skill to successfully complete it."

I chanced a glance at Owen, who appeared to be pouting in the chair next to me. His arms were folded across his chest, as if in a defensive posture, and there was a deep frown face as he looked at his feet.

David brought my attention back to him. "There are lives at stake here. A lot of them. We need you to be fully focused on the job. No more of your childish vendetta. No more sulking. Just the job. Expect further restrictions on your privileges when you return. My trust in you has been broken."

Forcing myself not to act wounded at his description of my behavior—after all, he was right—I tucked in my bottom lip and nodded.

"Fine. Do not disappoint me again, Mackenzie." The familiar words made me bristle, and his fatherly tone didn't help. I tried to shake off the feeling of discomfort. He might have been my father, but he'd missed most of my life. I didn't need his approval or disapproval. All I needed was to do my job.

"So, what's the job?" I asked, trying to sound confident.

"We've had several members of the Unseen working tirelessly to uncover more about Dux Ducis. Owen here is one of them. He's the one who actually discovered your target."

He didn't look up at the mention of his name. I knew because I was still staring at him.

Sensing something brewing, I asked, "If Owen's the one who found the guy, why isn't he looking into him? He probably knows the most about him."

"Because the man is considered highly dangerous. We feel you are best equipped to handle him."

The words pushed me back in my seat. Was that why he was mad? Did Owen want this job and resent me for taking it? "But I've only been here for a few months. Surely, Owen is—"

David cut me off. "If you're concerned you're stepping on his toes, that's not what he's upset about. We all agree you're the one for this job. Owen wants to go with you as your safety."

"Oh." It was as if all my breath had gone out of my lungs at once. Why would he want to go with me after what I'd done? "But after what I—"

"After what you did, we're not confident Owen can keep you under control, should something happen. Tracy will accompany you."

I looked over at Tracy, and she nodded. I chose to take it as an encouraging gesture.

"Back to the target. We've uncovered a plot against Coda."

Of all the ways I'd expected him to finish that sentence, he'd chosen the most unexpected. After all, it wasn't a major sporting event, a popular rock concert, a cruise ship, or anything like that. It was a highly intellectual gathering only known to those in the classical music community. Why target something like that? It wasn't like the general public would be directly affected.

"Why Coda?" I asked, trying to make sense of it.

"This year, over twenty thousand people are expected. I think the sheer numbers have attracted the Potestas' attention. Their motivation behind the attack is less obvious. Perhaps that's something you will discover."

Thinking of all the big names in today's classical musicians, I started to panic. "But some of the greatest musicians in the world will be there. Can you tell the organizers at FSU to cancel the event?"

"I've advised them to do so, but so far, they haven't. They don't believe we have enough evidence."

"What do you think the Potestas are planning?"

David took a breath. "Unfortunately, we think they're going to unleash the latest version of the chemical Dr. Jeppe developed."

"What?" It came out in an accusing hiss. "You can't let this happen."

"No, *you* can't let this happen. The man Owen found is thought to have a close connection with Dux Ducis. We need to uncover his identity so that we can do whatever it takes to stop this plot. If we don't…" He paused and looked straight into my eyes. "If *you* don't, tens of thousands of people will die."

A shudder ran through me as I thought of the screaming chimps. "And they won't die easily either."

"No, they won't. You need to get us as much information as quickly as possible so we can stop that from happening."

"Fine. When do we leave?" I looked over at Owen, assuming he would be helping Tracy and me on this one.

"Now. You'll take one of the cars to Atlanta as soon as you're ready. But Owen and the rest of the research team is staying here to search for further information."

I frowned, but I knew it wasn't the time to argue. "I'm ready."

As we left David's office, I realized I wasn't as ready as I thought. Owen hung back, and Tracy went on ahead, catching me between the two of them.

Tracy looked back when I stopped walking. "Go on ahead. I'll meet you at the car in twenty minutes." She nodded and left the gym.

Walking back to Owen, I tried to find words to say to him, but they wouldn't come. I kept hearing Mitchell's story in my mind. If he could forgive him, he could forgive me, right? But panic clawed at my gut. If I lost Owen… only then did it hit me how grave a loss that would be.

I didn't look at him when I approached, taking care to watch my feet as they closed the gap between us.

He let out a heavy sigh and folded me into his arms. I collapsed into him, but the words still didn't come.

"You are the worst kind of impossible."

"Which kind is that?" I asked, my words muffled by his neck and shoulder.

"The kind that is impossible to understand, impossible to

forgive, but impossible not to." He pulled back and looked at me with those beautiful brown eyes. The ones I fell in love with what seemed like ages ago. "The kind that's impossible to be without."

"Lucky for me," I said, incredulous that this man had decided I was worthy of him after everything I'd put him through. I had been so quick to turn my back on him for what he'd done. He had every right to do the same to me, but instead, he opened his arms.

He reached for something in his pocket. "I have something for you." He handed me my iPod.

I took it out and turned it over in my hand, unsure of what it meant.

"I took the liberty of adding the London Symphony Orchestra's latest recording of Gasbag de la Noot. I thought it might help you concentrate."

I held it in my hand, not closing my fingers around it. In that moment, a small shift happened in my mind. Maddie was still there, but I allowed all the other emotions, thoughts, and fears I'd been holding back into the forefront of my mind. I allowed Owen all the way back in. I wanted him in my future, I realized—and I actually *wanted* a future.

I closed my hand tightly around the object. "Thank you," I said, proud my voice didn't waver.

"You're welcome. Now go pack. It's over four hours to Atlanta, and you'll need it to read up on this guy."

I groaned. "Didn't I just get back from doing this?"

"No. You just got back from your dumb-ass vigilante mission. That was how you decided to use your vacation, so now you don't get one."

"Ah," I said, knowing there'd be more digs like that in my future. Somehow, it didn't bother me anymore, not now that I knew I'd been forgiven.

Leaning in, I didn't even think about what I was doing or what would happen if he didn't respond. All I was doing was saying goodbye to a man who loved me better than I had loved him. Silently, I vowed to change that as I kissed him deeply.

"Good luck," he said when we finally parted.

I nodded as I walked away, but I hoped we wouldn't need luck to carry us through the days ahead.

FIFTEEN

Dylan Shields didn't seem particularly special. Though Owen had done some pretty extensive detective work, he'd found very little information, which was suspicious in and of itself. What we did know was that Shields was a confirmed member of the Potestas with a connection with the University of Michigan. David hoped he was the link between Jeppe and Dux Ducis.

"Do you think this guy is even real? Are you sure he's not some sort of diversion they've cooked up to keep us busy? There aren't even the most basic facts about him. No birthdate, birthplace, parents, job, social security number, nothing. Do you think he's maybe a higher up that had his history erased?" I asked, thinking about Amanda. "How on Earth did our people track him to Atlanta, anyway?"

"One of our guys spotted him on some security camera footage. Some scouts we have stationed here confirmed the lead." She paused as she navigated the busy city streets. "And yes, he could be a diversion, but if so, what are they hiding behind him? We need to know," Tracy said.

"How can we hunt a diversion?"

"Yes. That part's tricky." She didn't once take her eyes off the road as we drove into downtown Atlanta. "Let's hope he's a higher up, then we'll really have a big score on our hands when we take him out."

It was shortly after lunchtime, and the research the Unseen had collected about Shields said he was regularly seen walking from Grady Memorial to Hurt Park at five thirty in the afternoon. After that, he seemed to disappear. It made absolutely no sense to me. Did he work at the hospital? If so, why wasn't there a record of him?

Not having much else to go on, we waited at the park. I grew more and more uneasy. "Tracy, this feels like a trap. There's nothing to go on. What if they've lured us here, lured me here?"

Tracy scanned our immediate surroundings suspiciously, but it wasn't unusual for her. "That's true, it could be. To be honest, I wish we'd brought more people with us."

She glanced at her watch. From a glance at my own, I knew we had about fifteen more minutes before we could expect our guest. "I'll stake him out first, okay? I'll just feel him out, try to get an idea of what we're in for."

"Sounds good." I breathed a sigh, relieved she was going to do some reconnaissance for me.

But a few minutes later, I noticed someone off in the distance that I couldn't hear at all. He was a total void. "Tracy," I whispered.

"I see him. He's not alone."

Sure enough, more and more voids popped up throughout the park. It felt like they were just materializing out of the ground. How had they learned to be so stealthy?

"What should we do?"

"Try not to get killed. That's our new objective. Forget the target for now. We're surrounded."

"Disguise yourself. Let them hear some inane thoughts so they don't know who you are," I said.

"What? That doesn't—"

I cut her off. "Just do it." They were starting to notice us. More than a few of them were throwing glances our way. There were a total of fifteen Potestas in the park, only three of them women, but there was still no sign of the man we knew as Shields.

Catching the eye of another member of the Potestas, I sent out a thought. *Man, it's gorgeous today. I'm sure glad we decided to take our break out here. Jeez, what is he looking at? I'll bet he thinks I'm checking him out just because I made eye contact. Men are such pigs.*

I hoped the standoffish approach would work with this group. I didn't want to do anything to provoke a direct inter-action—that sort of thing would likely get us caught. Looking back down at the book I'd brought to make it look like I was out there to enjoy the nice day, I risked saying something to Tracy.

"Are you doing it?"

"Yes." She also kept her face angled toward her magazine, but I knew her well enough to realize she was keeping constant tabs on those around us.

I read the words on the page in my head, making sure everyone around me could hear them. Then I saw him. It broke my train of thought for just an instant, and I glanced around to make sure no one had noticed.

With one eye on Shields and the other on my book, I watched him walk down the path right in front of us. He didn't seem to be walking toward any specific person, just meandering. Taking a seat at a bench not fifteen yards from us, he ate a sandwich he must've picked up on the way over.

It was frustrating not to be able to get into his mind right then, but clearly, this was much bigger than we'd guessed. Fifteen Potestas didn't gather around for nothing.

For a very tense ten minutes, I watched him eat his sandwich as I absently read my book. I didn't risk speaking to Tracy again.

Once his last bite was gone, he got up, tossed the wrappings in the trash, and retraced his steps back out of the park, walking right past us yet again.

After he left, the Potestas slowly trickled out after him. It took another ten minutes or so for the last of them to leave the area. I let out a breath I hadn't realized I was holding.

"Holy shit," I said. "Tracy, we need more help."

She already had her phone out. "I couldn't agree more," she said as she typed out a message.

The following day, Owen, Mitchell, Camden, and most of the rest of our division of the Unseen met us for breakfast in the hotel. Tracy reserved a special meeting room for us to eat in, so we could talk freely.

Owen embraced me long and hard, and I squeezed him back, finally letting myself feel how scared I'd been. Hell, I was *still* scared. We didn't exchange words; we just looked at each other with gratitude in our eyes.

It took a few minutes for everyone to exchange greetings. *We might stand a chance*, I thought as people started to settle around the huge, oval table at the center of the room. We had a fair number of mind readers in our army, and there was at least one of us for every Potesta. Owen stayed right by my side as we got some cereal from the buffet that had been set up along the edge of the conference room and took our seats at the table.

"What's our approach?" Owen asked once everyone was settled.

"The park isn't very big," I said through a bite of Froot Loops. "If we all go down there, they'll notice us, don't you think? Not to mention, they all saw Tracy and me down there yesterday. They'll think something is up."

"Well, you guys have already passed their test because you were able to act like you enjoyed taking your break out there. But you have a point for the rest of us," Camden said.

"Well, we could take turns milling around the park. Just have a revolving door, so to speak. Plus, you could hide two or three people up in the trees throughout the park," Owen said.

The wheels turned in my head. "If Tracy and I are out of sight, they won't know they should be hearing thoughts from us. Right?" A few heads nodded at me. "Tracy, we're idiots. Why didn't we do that yesterday?"

She shook her head. "I'm glad we didn't. This goes deeper than we thought. We needed help. I hope we have enough."

Mitchell spoke up. "Tracy said you've learned an interesting defense technique for keeping the Potestas distracted. She said it saved your lives yesterday."

"I guess. I kind of assumed it was what you all did to hide yourselves from them. Just let them hear some stupid, normal thoughts About the last sports game, or some girl you're dating, or some made-up problem at work. Just make yourself seem normal to distract them. It worked on Washington, and it worked on fifteen Potestas yesterday, so I'd say it's fairly effective."

Everyone nodded as they considered the various scenarios we'd laid out for the day ahead. But I still had questions. "If that's not how you've kept yourselves hidden among the Potestas before, how do you normally do it?"

Tracy shrugged as she chewed her bacon. "We didn't, really. Usually, it's a race to get in—and out—before we're noticed. But this technique offers a whole new level of time and safety for us. You saved our skins yesterday, and I imagine your tactics will save many more of us in the years to come."

We all chewed on our breakfast for a moment, trying to piece together a plan. Finally, I said, "So, how about this? Tracy and I will hide in the trees while the rest of you will mill around, keeping us safe."

"No. Absolutely not. That's too dangerous because of the level of relaxation required of the body to enter someone else's mind. They could fall out and kill themselves," Owen piped up.

Then, the idea hit me. "What if we tie ourselves up there? We have plenty of time to get into position. If we go down there now, hours before he's expected, we'll be golden. You guys would be down there to keep an eye on us." Excitement at the prospect made me talk faster and faster. I looked up into the faces of my brothers and sisters in arms. "This could work."

"People will be suspicious of what we're doing. I'm pretty sure people don't normally tie each other up in trees," Mitchell offered.

He was right. "We'll have to deal with whatever attention we attract. I mean, there's not too many ways you can tie someone up in a tree without being seen by someone."

Tracy and I were set up in our trees about two hours later. It took some time to find a hardware store where we could buy rope, hooks sturdy enough to satisfy Owen's concerns about our safety, and a ladder for those responsible for tying us up there.

In the end, I was glad we were there so early. It was quite a production to get ourselves up in the trees. In fact, we were spotted by a police officer just as Owen was securing the last hook and knot.

"Just what do you think you're doing?"

Owen froze, but I smiled at her.

"Just setting up for a little game," I said, easing into her unprotected mind so I could urge her to move on.

"Oh. Well, have fun," she said and walked away.

"You are just the absolute worst kind of impossible," Owen said as he leaned in to kiss me. "Good luck. I'll be milling around down below if you need anything."

"I'll see you on the other side of this mess," I said, already looking forward to completing the mission.

The hours in that tree passed slowly. I kicked myself for not bringing that book I'd pretended to read the day before, anything to keep my mind occupied and make the time pass a little faster. The tree wasn't exactly the most comfortable place to sit for more than a few minutes, let alone six hours.

But the time eventually passed, as it always inevitably does. From behind the tree's branches, I noticed the same faces come trickling in, but I couldn't risk signaling any of my fellow Unseen. I could only hope they'd noticed and were doing their jobs. Soon, I was reassured as they started to trickle through the park. The block prevented me from hearing their defensive thoughts, but based on the way the Potestas essentially ignored them, I could tell it was working.

Right on time, Shields took his seat on the bench across from the tree where I was stationed, and I could only hope Tracy had begun her attack. The plan was to let her hack into his mind and make her presence known. This, in theory, would distract him, giving me the chance to get in cleanly and unnoticed. Hopefully, she would simply be pushed out unharmed and I could poke around undetected. But as I sat in the tree, waiting for my turn at Shields, I thought of what Mitchell had told me about these people. They would never just push her out unharmed. Regret and dread settled in, and I wanted to cry out, to do anything and everything I could to keep her safe and protected. But it was too late. I had to focus. There were a lot of lives in my hands. I couldn't let my panic allow them to slip through my fingers.

I took a deep breath as I counted the seconds, and the five minutes I waited dragged on like an eternity. Then, I pressed my attack.

Immediately, I felt his struggle with Tracy. She wasn't getting pushed out easily, that was for sure. Lucky for me, she was keeping him so occupied that I slipped right in. His defenses weren't even active, which puzzled me. I'd thought that, once set up, a person's defenses were always armed and ready to go. But his were like traps that had already been sprung, perhaps by Tracy? I made a mental note to ask her about it later as I pressed onward.

His mind seemed strangely empty as I began to search it for information. Another tactic of the Potestas, I assumed. Redoubling my efforts, I combed through the darkness until I came across something. It was nothing more than a speck at first. But as I got closer, I knew it was the jackpot, or at least something that would lead me to the jackpot.

Under my focused attention, the speck became clearer and more distinct. It was a model train. Picking it up, I examined it more closely. It was an exact replica of the SunRail—the train on which my best friend had died. My mouth went dry as I peered inside the small windows. I didn't want to watch Maddie die again. I'd already glazed over it from Washington's perspective. But I couldn't stop it. No matter what I did, I couldn't control what I was seeing.

Washington was sitting next to Maddie, flirting with her. Actually flirting. The rage nearly made me crush the model in my hands. Two other men—both Potestas—had taken up positions next to her and across from her. All of them were engaging her in friendly banter as they waited for the train to start up. Maddie ate up their attention, flirting right back. And who could blame her? They were all very attractive, and I knew from experience that Washington was quite the charmer.

Two of them got up eventually. One excused himself to check something in his bag. Washington said he wanted to go to the restroom before the train left, but he added that he couldn't wait to come back to Maddie's beautiful face. She beamed at him, and I wanted to walk him in front of that bus all over again. I watched helplessly as the last man sweet-talked Maddie, and then the train's explosion blew my heart to pieces.

SIXTEEN

The model train lay in pieces at my feet. The explosion had not harmed me at all. It wasn't real, at least, not this time. I looked around in the darkness, tears streaming down my face, when something tugged at the back of my mind.

Two men had left the train. The one who stayed had died with Maddie. So whose memory had I just watched?

The sound of someone clapping echoed through the space, but I couldn't find the source of the noise.

"Well done, Mackenzie." A man's voice slithered through the air around me, making my skin crawl.

Folding my arms over my chest and pulling my sweater tight around me, I tried to protect myself from him.

"You are a rare specimen indeed." I had to resist the urge to cover my ears when he spoke. Was it Shields? I wasn't sure who else it could be, so by default, I assumed it had to be. "Your skills are like nothing I've ever seen before, not even among our most advanced members." He made a tsking sound. "Too bad we didn't find you first."

"You would've killed me if you had, considering who I am. Then you never would've known I was such a *rare specimen*," I spat.

The voice laughed. "I can't argue that. But I think it's fair to say that we've learned our lesson. We'd like to have you for our side. We believe you would be a very valuable asset. In fact, we've been looking for you for quite some time. I had no idea we'd be lucky enough to have you walk right into our latest meeting."

"A meeting." I said it as a statement, not a question. "Of course. That's why so many of you keep gathering here."

"And yet, you still attempted to get what you came for. Very brave of you."

"Or stupid," I said.

The voice chuckled. "A sense of humor to boot. Like I said, you're a valuable asset."

"I've been hearing that a lot lately."

Again, he laughed. "I bet you have."

The voice was quiet, as if he actually expected me to consider his offer. It was my turn to laugh. "You are all dumber than I thought."

"Are we?" His tone didn't seem to show any sign that I'd wounded him.

"I'm not joining you. I've seen what that chemical can do, the suffering it would cause. I don't want any part of it." By that point, I'd had enough. I tried to break the connection, but alarmingly, I couldn't. Opening my eyes seemed like a Herculean task. In fact, I had trouble even connecting to my own body. Before my alarm could develop into a full-blown panic, he interrupted my attempts to escape.

"I'm sorry to hear that." His tone turned dark, making the panic shooting through my body all the more insistent. "Those who are not with us are against us." Slowly, I perceived the smallest bit of light, a short distance off. I saw Tracy lying in a heap just under the light source.

I ran to her and collapsed by her side. "Tracy," I whispered. "We have to get out. We're done here. Let's go." But she didn't respond. Shaking her shoulder, I pleaded with her again. "Come on."

Just then, the voice started laughing—quietly at first, and then with a maniacal power that made me shake.

Owen and the others. My mind started to race as their faces popped into view. How could I warn them? Tell them the mission had failed? But trying to help might compromise their position. *So I just let them flounder?* No. I couldn't just sit idly by, letting them get slaughtered.

Tracy. I may not have been able to find my own body, but Tracy was right here. It blurred the lines between the mind and reality, but I couldn't get hung up on technicalities. I had to try.

Ignoring the laughter that grew louder with every breath I took, I tried to infiltrate her mind, but I found only fog.

"Tracy?" I called out. "Tracy! You have to warn them. I think we might die, but you can save the rest of them. You have to call out to them. Do it! Now!" I took a deep breath and yelled. "Owen, run!"

But without any warning, I was thrown headlong out of her mind. When I opened my eyes, I was lying on top of Tracy's crumpled body. I looked more closely at her. She lay on her side, knees drawn up, her blonde hair spilling every which way. Her face seemed peaceful, relaxed, and almost unrecognizable.

"What have you done to her?" I asked the darkness.

"I've eliminated her. She wasn't useful."

"You *what?*" My heart pounded in my ears as I turned her onto her back and pressed my ear to her chest, willing there to be a sound. But all I could hear was the man's laughter.

"Shut up!" I screamed until my voice was hoarse. I began chest compressions on the lifeless image of her body, not knowing how much good it would do, but I couldn't just let her lie there. Was she still tied to the tree? Had Owen and the others saved her? I could only hope as I pounded on her chest.

"Your efforts are as commendable as they are useless. I've commanded her to stop breathing, and so she has."

"You're... an... idiot," I said between compressions. "Do you know how much information she had on the Unseen? You've pissed away countless secrets, all in an effort to what? Scare me? Intimidate me? Show me how superior you are and how unworthy the Unseen are?"

He didn't laugh like I thought he would. But he didn't bring her back to life either. Instead, he let me sit in silence as I pounded on the chest of my lifeless friend, wondering how I'd come to find myself in this new and terrible version of hell.

SEVENTEEN

The voice did not return. I had no way of marking time in the darkness, and even if I did, time passed differently in the mind than it did in the real world.

Tracy's body hadn't faded with the voice, and I continued to give her CPR until exhaustion finally overwhelmed me. I gave in to the tears and collapsed on her chest.

"I'm sorry, Tracy. I knew we shouldn't go in, but it was too late by the time I realized it. I couldn't stop you without endangering everyone else. It's my fault. I'm sorry."

But her lifeless body had nothing to say. No reprimands. No *stop your blubbering*—nothing but silence.

I didn't have anything to cover her with, so I couldn't shield myself from the reality of her death. Folding her arms over her chest, I tried to make her look comfortable again, at peace. But I knew better. I knew she'd died horribly, and it was my fault. I tried not to think about what Shields might have done to her, how he'd probably tortured her, but the darkness didn't offer many distractions.

After a time, I found myself wishing the voice would've taken her with him. As soon as the thought formed, I regretted it. Once she was gone, I would never see her again. But this wasn't even her. It was a shell of who she'd once been.

Regret became my companion for a little while, simply because there was no room in my heart for more grief. So I blamed myself. I shouldn't have agreed to this mission. I wasn't ready or prepared. I had too many distractions on my mind, too many burdens on my heart. I was too new. Maybe with more training, more skill, I could have succeeded, but I'd ruined everything instead.

Because of me, the Unseen had lost one of their most valuable members. Tracy was the best of the best. What on Earth would we do without her?

Once the questions started, there was no stopping them. How could I have prevented her death? What could I have done differently? The number of Potestas milling around should've been a clue that we couldn't handle the job. But if we couldn't, who could?

When the answers didn't come, I got up and ventured away from Tracy. Now that I knew I couldn't save her, it was time for me to once again search for either a way out or a way into the mind that had trapped me. I struck out in a random direction and just put one foot in front of the other, always keeping the light source at my back. Strangely though, no matter what I did, I couldn't make much progress in distancing myself from it. I could hear my shoes hitting the floor, so I knew I was walking, but the space between Tracy's body and me never seemed to grow any larger.

After a while, I gave up and went back to her. Sitting down beside her, I decided a more internal approach might work better. Taking a deep breath, I tried to calm my racing thoughts. What had become of Owen and the others? Did they manage to get out? Did my warning work? What if Owen had been killed right alongside Tracy? What if all the others were gone?

No, I thought, taking another deep breath and making myself lightheaded. *Get out. That's what you need to focus on doing. You're no use to anyone trapped in this bizarre purgatory. Just concentrate on getting out.*

Hoping to shut out the few distractions that surrounded me, I closed my eyes and searched for myself. It was an odd feeling, being so separated from my body. I knew I still existed, that somewhere on Earth I was still breathing, but I didn't know where, when, or how. I had no idea if I was still tied to that tree in the park, if they'd moved me someplace, or if Owen or one of the others had rescued my body and I was safely back at the facility.

No. I sent out the questions swirling in my mind. But I couldn't stop the rising desperation that held the peace I sought just out of reach. That was when the if-onlys started to plague me. If only I'd saved Tracy, if only I'd left Owen and the others out of this, if only I'd... what? What else could I have done to prevent this situation? And what could I now do to fix it?

The answers continued to evade me, and, suddenly, a voice interrupted my thoughts. A voice I'd recognize anywhere. A voice I'd been listening to for over eighteen years.

"Ah, Mackenzie. I'd like to say it's good to see you again, but I never did much care for you," Amanda said.

My mouth hung open as a giant image of her was projected against the darkness.

She occupied most of the frame. Her makeup was precisely applied—not too much, just enough to make her look polished. She looked exactly as I remembered her, but there was something in her expression I'd never seen before. Was she happy? What was she happy about? Had she wormed her way into the man's mind to save me?

Then another question occurred to me. Could I address her directly?"

"Hello..." I trailed off, not sure what to call her. We both knew she wasn't my aunt. She didn't respond, so I had no idea if she'd even heard me.

"Perhaps I should explain the... situation before we get into why you're here. I don't expect you to understand because honestly, I don't think you're capable, but I'll tell you anyway. I've left the Unseen. After squandering my life with them, I was offered a rather high position with the Potestas. Given the amount of inside knowledge I had about you, they were happy to forgive my transgressions and accept me into their ranks."

Her brown, perfectly styled, shoulder-length hair bobbed as she shrugged. "The Potestas take very good care of me. I have everything I could ever want. And I'm able to use my abilities to their fullest extent. The Potestas can do things the Unseen are too backward to even imagine. Naturally, I was more than happy to join them after the way I'd been treated by the Unseen."

David was right again, I thought.

Narrowing my eyes at the projection, I walked closer to it, trying to get a feel for what I was seeing. Her image was bigger than life, and as I walked closer, I had to look up to see her face. Was it a recording, or was I watching this live through Shields' eyes?

She appeared to be inside, but the frame was so entirely filled by her image, I couldn't discern much else. As she shifted in her seat, I thought I caught a glimpse of something behind her, but I couldn't tell exactly what.

"Now…" A smile crept across Amanda's face—a rare expression for her. "I can let you in on a little secret. I think you're familiar with a gathering called Coda?"

I shifted my weight, growing more and more uncomfortable with the direction this conversation was going.

"Of course you are. You always dreamed of going to it. Even had the gall to ask me to fund a little excursion for you and that pathetic friend of yours."

"Now wait just a minute—" I said, unable to sit silently while she prattled on unchecked.

But she interrupted me, and I still couldn't tell if I was even being heard. "At any rate, I'm sure you know some of the details of our plan. You know what we've allowed you to know— enough to make the Unseen panic, but not enough for them to do anything about it. It's actually quite entertaining to watch you all scramble.

"But, I'm getting off track. Dux Ducis was a trap, a made-up role played by Dylan here, a few others, and me. That idiot scientist had no idea what Dylan was doing when he planted the defenses, nor did he know Dylan was one of the ones playing Dux Ducis. Not only were we able to control Jeppe with the alias, but the person we created was untraceable, and he led you right where we wanted you.

"Our plans for Coda are merely a test run, you see. Nothing more than a distraction for the Unseen while we plan strategic, global distribution of the chemical we're calling Zero. I don't want to give you all the details—after all, the surprise is half the fun—but Zero will help put our organization into the ultimate position of power."

Strategic, global distribution? Position of power?

As I contemplated what she'd said, the frame panned out, revealing more of the room my former aunt occupied. A person sat just behind her, a woman. A woman who looked a lot like me. Her likeness startled me so much that I choked, halting the tears in their tracks.

Soon, a second projection appeared. It was fuzzy at first, and it blinked in and out a few times before becoming clear. I glanced over at the first projection and saw that my former aunt was taking a seat in front of the woman.

"You, Mackenzie, are going to play a large part in this plot, whether you like it or not." She smiled again, but it was a wicked smile, full of evil.

I looked again at the woman who was near my former aunt. Suddenly, I realized she was wearing the same outfit my physical body had last worn. In fact, I was still wearing it. *That can't be me... can it?*

My eyes darted back to the second projection, struggling to make sense of it. This image was much blurrier, and it continued to blink in and out rapidly. Still, I could make out a seated figure.

Returning my gaze to the original projection, I narrowed in on the mess of dark hair obstructing the face of the mystery woman. I reached up and touched my own messy hair. Desperation overtook me as I frantically glanced back and forth between the two screens, trying to convince myself that what I knew to be true wasn't.

The original projection panned around, so that its new vantage point was behind my former aunt. "You are our greatest weapon, you see." She looked at the woman sitting across from her, who was motionless except for the steady rise and fall of her shoulders.

Dread filled my body the way water fills a cup. It rose from the pit of my stomach until I was nearly choking on it as the original screen got closer and closer to the girl—the weapon. I couldn't look away.

Then my face filled the screen, and no amount of denial would erase it. They had me. They'd captured my body. I railed at the screen, thrashing and tearing at the image, but nothing happened. The terrible truth lay there before me.

Now what did they plan to do with it? As if on cue, my former aunt began explaining my part in their horrible plot.

"That day when you thought you could pull one over on Shields here," the second projection showed Shields' face, while the first still showed my own. Slowly, I pieced together what was happening. The first had to be what Shields could see, and the second displayed my own line of vision. "I couldn't be more pleased. David's arrogance about your skills played to our advantage. Perhaps if he had waited, let you hone your skills a bit more, let you sort out your… issues, you would've been more formidable. But because your focus was so," she searched for the right word, "divided, we took you easily."

Shields cleared his throat.

"Well, perhaps easily isn't the right word. At any rate, you're ours now. After a carefully choreographed struggle, we allowed the others to escape, but not without damage," she said through another smile that made another scream tickle the back of my throat as I struggled to keep my mouth shut.

"And now, you will help us defeat the Unseen for good."

I collapsed to the ground in front of the two projections, unable to bear the weight of the freight train barreling down on me.

"You will be sent back into their facility. You will tell them exactly what we want you to tell them, and in so doing, you'll help us pull off our attack on Coda, as well as our later, larger attacks. And we will wipe out your little friends while we're at it. You will get the Unseen in position, and then you will mysteriously disappear to safety. You will be where we want, when we want."

My former aunt leaned back in her chair, a satisfied smile on her face "You're on our side now, Mackenzie, whether you like it or not. And even better, you'll get to watch your friends die." Her laughter followed her footsteps as she walked out of the room, and the original projection went dark, leaving me alone with the empty shell of myself.

EIGHTEEN

The despair I felt was difficult to describe. It was more than hopelessness.

Looking over at Tracy's body, I asked, "What do I do? How can I fix this?"

She just lay there like she was sleeping. "Tracy!" I yelled. "People's lives are at stake here. A lot of people's lives. What should I do? How could I stop this?"

Silence answered me again. Sighing wearily, I turned away from her lifeless body. "I don't know either."

At first, I ran, hoping I could outpace the darkness. But when that didn't happen, I ran out of steam.

Then I started to walk. I put one foot in front of the other, just to be doing something. My mind alternately was filled with everything and nothing. One moment, it swirled with worries— Owen, David, Mitchell, the Unseen, Coda, and the people of the world—the next, it was totally blank as I wandered aimlessly in the depths of Shields' mind.

The darkness was odd. There was nothing but blackness all around me, and yet, I could still see myself and where I was walking. It never seemed to change no matter how far I walked. But I never turned back to check on my progress. Really, I didn't want to know. Besides, I wasn't trying to escape. Well, maybe that wasn't entirely true. I wasn't trying to escape Shields; I was trying to escape myself. I needed to get away, get some peace, so I could figure out what to do next.

After what felt like days of walking, the darkness finally began to lift. The sun rose across a beautiful white sand beach with crystal clear waters lapping gently at its edge. The sound of the waves calmed my despairing mind and drew me closer. I took off my shoes and socks so I could curl my toes in the sugary sand.

I still didn't turn around. I didn't need to see the blackness that haunted me. I knew it was there, and although I didn't understand this unexpected respite I'd found, I couldn't help but embrace it.

Dipping my foot in the deliciously warm water, I decided to wade in. I didn't bother taking off my clothes; I just kept walking in until the water closed over my head. Slowly letting the air out of my lungs, I sank to the sandy bottom and sat, letting the current rock me back and forth. I wanted to stay there. Let the ocean take me. End it. At least that way I'd be free, and the others would be safe.

But, defiantly, my lungs demanded air. For a moment, I ignored them, reminding them that this wasn't real, that they didn't need air because they had plenty of it wherever the Potestas were keeping me. But eventually, their screaming became louder than the screaming in my mind. Even then, I paused, letting the sound in my head drown out my problems. But instinct finally took over and I broke to the surface, gasping for air.

Reluctantly, I trudged back to the beach, feeling no better than I had before. I'd hoped for some kind of cleansing, some kind of epiphany when I walked into the sea. But there had been nothing. There was no rescue for me.

Dripping wet but not cold, I walked toward the dunes. As I crested them, I saw a beautiful meadow of wildflowers spread out before me. It was at once a lovely and odd juxtaposition of scenery. A clear lake sat quietly off to one side while a huge snowcapped mountain cast a lovely reflection on the water. And there, at the edge of the lake, sat a lovely little log cabin. Longing to rest, I walked through the field of color toward my shelter.

As I got closer, I realized part of the cabin actually extended out over the water. Before going inside, I walked out onto the deck and sat dangling my toes in the water. It was cold, much colder than the ocean I'd just come from, but not uncomfortable. Sitting there, I pleaded for the peace that surrounded me to overtake my mind. When it didn't, I reluctantly decided to explore.

The interior of the cabin was everything I'd ever wanted in a home without realizing it. The huge entryway opened into a living room area, complete with a baby grand piano. How long had it been since I'd sat at the bench? Too long. I stroked the keys longingly, wondering if I had the courage to play.

Not now, I thought as I looked around the cabin. It had looked small from the outside, but inside, it was spacious. Windows lined almost every wall, providing lovely views of the meadow, the lake, and the mountain. I ventured upstairs and found the bedroom. The bed was huge and inviting with plush bedding and at least a dozen pillows. But before I could collapse into it and let the darkness take me, I walked over to the window. From that vantage point, I could see the gently rolling waves of the beach just beyond the edges of the meadow. It was lovely, odd, and perfect all at the same time.

"What is this place?" I asked aloud.

"It's your own personal paradise," the voice answered. After being in silence for so long, the sound startled me.

"My what?" I looked around the room. It was true. Right down to the personal touches. A guitar sat near the bed, and there was a keyboard on the other side of the room. Both looked identical to my own instruments. The walls were decorated with abstract pictures of instruments and framed sheet music. Bold reds and blacks accented the soft white linens on the bed. It was a perfect retreat for me, complete with a to-die-for view.

Was that what had happened? Had I died? But how could this be heaven if that voice was there with me?

"We thought we might as well keep you comfortable during your imprisonment."

My imprisonment. So I wasn't free, and I wasn't dead. I'd accomplished nothing in my wanderings. The rage that had been building inside me since I first saw my own face in that projection finally boiled over.

I picked up the guitar by the neck and swung it, sending the lamp on the bedside table flying. Again and again, I swung the guitar until it was toothpicks. Then I picked up the keyboard and smashed the windows with it, turning next on the beautiful cherry wood dresser and mirror, the bookshelves lining the walls, anything within my line of sight. Seeing a shard of glass, I picked it up and went to work on the bedding, shredding it into ribbons.

As the feathers flew, a picture on the ground caught my eye. The glass in the frame was broken, but the image behind remained untouched. Maddie had her arm around me, and she was giving me a broad smile. I wore an equally joyful expression. The piece of glass fell from my miraculously undamaged hand, and I held the picture tightly. I ran my thumb across Maddie's face, needing her help, wondering how I'd gotten so lost so fast in her absence. My rage dissolved into sadness, and silent tears coursed their way down my cheeks as I stared at her face.

"And that's why you'll never escape. I don't even have to work to keep you here," the voice said, chuckling softly. "You'll do it for me."

"What does that mean?" I asked, but his laughter drowned out my words.

As it faded, the projection screen returned. It wasn't Shields' point of view I was seeing—it was my own. I was walking, rather stiffly, across the parking lot to the facility of the Unseen.

Horrified, I watched as I easily passed through all the facility's outer security measures and slipped inside. And why not? I belonged there.

It's begun, I thought. *And there's not a damn thing you can do except watch the world come crashing down around you.*

NINETEEN

s I went deeper and deeper into the facility, I held my breath, knowing I shouldn't be there, but I was powerless to stop it. I couldn't control my own body, and in that moment, I realized how terrible Washington's fate had been.

The voice came back when I made it to the main floor. "Congratulations. You have officially gotten us deeper into enemy territory than any other agent in history."

"Fuck you," I said through gritted teeth as I watched myself, glued to the projection.

Across the room, Owen was slouched lazily on the couch, watching a movie. His arm was in a sling, and his face was black and blue in places, but he was alive, as were the others who sat near him. Mitchell and Camden both caught sight of me before Owen did, but they let him greet me first.

He got up, grimacing only slightly, and ran to me. Cinching me to him with his one good arm, he didn't speak for a few moments as the others gathered around. Owen's breath was coming in short gasps, and I struggled to hold it together. *That's not me*, I wanted to scream. *Get away from her!* Anything to make him understand the horror that was about to befall him and the others. Instead, I just watched it happen, like a soap opera on television.

As he hugged me, I noticed my body didn't relax into him

like it usually did. I remained stiff as a board as Owen and the others shared an outpouring of emotion.

"What happened?" Owen finally asked me.

"They let me go." The words were just as robotic as my movements, and I couldn't help but laugh. Surely, my friends would see through this act.

Owen's voice brought my attention back to the screen. "What do you mean, they let you go?"

"They let me go," I repeated in the same robotic tone.

Mitchell stepped forward and took a long look into my eyes. He scrutinized me in a way that sparked a tiny bit of hope. Climbing down off the bed, I moved closer to the projection.

"Mitchell," I whispered.

His eyes narrowed as he looked right at me on the screen. Frowning, he pulled back and mumbled something into Owen's ear.

Owen nodded and took the robot's hand. I looked down at my hand, empty and cold in the destroyed room, and then looked back to the projection half a world away.

Owen led me down to David's office, with a few of the others in tow. If he noticed any stiffness in my gait, he didn't comment on it.

Part of me hoped my body would fall down the stairs if it kept walking like that, ending this farce once and for all. That way, none of my friends would have to die. Unfortunately for me, we made it to the bottom.

Owen didn't even knock before he went into David's office.

"David. It's good to see you," I said in that strange, stiff voice. But it wasn't me; it was them playing their sadistic little game. He looked up at me from some file he was poring over. His face was haggard, with dark bags under his eyes and a five o'clock shadow that looked more like an eleven o'clock shadow.

"Mackenzie." It came out like an exhalation as he rushed over and took me in his arms. He'd never hugged me before, and I could tell the robot didn't respond. I didn't see my hands go around his neck or torso or anything. I just stood there, letting him hug me.

David didn't seem to notice. "What happened to you?" he asked as he pulled back and helped me into one of the chairs in front of his desk. He sat on his desk and faced me while Owen took the seat next to mine.

"They let me go." It sounded exactly the same the third time as it had the first two. There'd been no change in tone or inflection, and the statement hadn't become any smoother with practice.

"Why?"

I didn't answer.

I couldn't believe it. They hadn't worked out even the simplest of cover stories? Or were they having more trouble controlling my body than they'd expected? I wasn't sure which option to hope for. Either way, the odds seemed to be tipping slightly in my favor.

David leaned forward and looked deep into my eyes. I hoped they appeared as vacant as they actually were. He was my father. He would see, wouldn't he?

"Mackenzie, the Potestas don't just let people go. What happened?"

"I don't remember." I saw David glance doubtfully at Owen, who frowned in response.

"Owen, how did she get here? Did you see a car? Where did she come from?"

Owen shook his head. "I don't know. She just appeared in the living room. We were watching a movie, and I looked up to see her standing there as still as a statue."

"This is ridiculous," I shouted at the projection. "David! David! Don't tell her anything! It's a trap! David! Look at me! Don't you see?"

"Mackenzie, are you okay?" The robot didn't respond, so he went further. "Your eye is twitching."

Apparently, my body must have brought my hand to my eye and rubbed it, because half the screen went dark. *My eye twitched*, I thought. Had I done that? Could I use it to communicate with them?

"Maybe I can help fill in the gaps for you," he started.

Caught in my snare, I screamed hopelessly and helplessly at David to stop talking, not to tell them anything, but the robot me just kept rubbing my eye.

Yes, keep rubbing that eye, I thought, willing David to notice, but he didn't.

"We believe Shields was a more formidable foe than we anticipated," David said.

"Well *duh*," I shouted, making the robot take another swipe at her eye.

"Do you need some eye drops or something?" David asked, veering from his story.

Yes! He's noticing.

But the robot didn't respond. Apparently, that question was outside her script.

Letting out a tense breath, he continued on with his explanation, adding to my frustration. "He managed to take out Tracy somehow." He paused, searching my face for a reaction to the news that my friend and colleague had died. The robot gave no such response. He cleared his throat and started to continue, but Owen piped up.

"We could tell something was wrong. Tracy called out for me to run, and then shit hit the fan. The other members of the Potestas who were milling around ambushed us. A bunch of us managed to get away by using your defensive technique. But I couldn't leave you. Mitchell and I tried to get you down, but they flanked us, ten against two. I told Mitchell to run, and he did, so he managed to get away fairly unscathed. I wasn't so lucky. But they let me live."

"Strangely," David added. "This whole thing is a bit strange." He circled his desk and sat down heavily in the huge, executive-style chair. "Why kill Tracy and no one else? And it's not at all like them to let two members of our ranks go free, particularly one as high profile as you, Mackenzie."

"To be fair, we did get a few good shots in. Camden had no trouble taking out the guy who tried to get him. It was a little comical actually. This puny little white guy ran at him like he thought he was going to best him in hand-to-hand combat or something. Camden clotheslined him, and then tried to take control of his mind. When he didn't have any luck, he moved on."

"Camden couldn't take control of some puny punk?" I asked, but of course, they couldn't hear me from my prison.

"Your tactics with the Unseen are a bit… primitive," the voice said.

"So, you *are* still there," I said, a smile spreading across my face. The voice went silent again, but I didn't need him to respond. I knew he was there.

For some reason, that gave me hope. Maybe he knew his little scheme wasn't working and he was pissed. For as ill equipped as Shields and my former aunt seemed to think the Unseen were, I knew the truth. Someone would notice something was wrong. All I had to do was wait.

"At any rate, while they were busy with me, they must've taken you away." Owen's voice was quiet and distant. I sensed his guilt, and I wanted so desperately to reach for him, to tell him I was okay, even if I wasn't. But the betrayer didn't do any of those things. She simply sat stock-still, looking back and forth between the two men in the office with her.

David picked up the story then. "You were gone for over two weeks. We thought you…" He hesitated, clearly not wanting to say what they'd thought. "Well, at any rate, I'm certainly glad we were wrong."

"You shouldn't be," I said aloud, but only the voice heard me.

"You're right about that," it said.

Something about what David had said caught me. *Two weeks.* I tried to calculate in my head what that meant—what date it had to be—but I was having trouble keeping up.

Then, my own voice, delivered by the robot, interrupted my train of thought. "Coda."

"Yes," David responded. "We've made very little progress there."

"They have a mole in the faculty. They will release the chemical called Zero. Find them to stop it." I was speechless.

The betrayer, the robot, was leading them all to their deaths.

"*Nooo!*" I screamed. "Don't listen to her! You'll all die." The projection cut in and out, as if the robot was blinking rapidly, but David didn't notice. He was too preoccupied with what the robot had said.

David's eyes first went wide at the implications of my words, and then narrowed as he thought about it. "How is it that you remember this little tidbit and not what happened to you?"

The betrayer sat there silently and stared back at David. He didn't look away.

"Good! Keep challenging her, David! Don't believe a word of it!" I cheered.

"Coda is starting tomorrow, Mackenzie. We don't have time to research which faculty member might be a mole. We need to save our men for the larger picture. I sense something more is going on here."

"More than the potential deaths of more than twenty thousand people?" Owen's voice startled me. "David, we can't just let them die."

"It's Professor Marcia Peterson." I blanched at betrayer robot's words.

"How far are you planning to take this? How many people in my life are going to die at your hands?" I asked the voice.

"All of them."

TWENTY

"**P**rofessor Peterson? Are you sure? Wasn't she your mentor?" Owen asked, clearly a little shocked.

"It's her. Find her and destroy the plot against Coda." It wasn't a sentence that should've been spoken with such a flat tone. There should have been some force behind it, some passion.

Owen noticed, and he took a long look at the betrayer before turning to David. "What do you think? I can go and nip this in the bud today. You won't even have to send anyone else."

"Professor Peterson is more dangerous than you might think. You'll need back up. How do you expect to remove all the Zero by yourself?" the betrayer asked.

David exhaled. "If Zero, as you call it, is on campus, we are not equipped to remove it. We would call in a team of specialists to clean it up. *If* we go today, we go with a small group. Our goal would be to gather enough evidence to get the faculty to cancel the event."

I couldn't help but feel hopeful; David was skeptical—I knew him well enough to see it on his face.

"What do you mean, if?" Owen asked.

David turned to the robot. "Mackenzie, would you please excuse us? I know you must be exhausted. Why don't you go relax for a bit? Owen will join you shortly."

Owen watched the robot closely for a reaction, but evidently, she showed none. She didn't address either of them as she stood and left the room. I thought she would keep walking all the way to her room, like a good little robot, but she didn't. She left the door to David's office the tiniest bit ajar and stood outside listening.

"She's still there!" I yelled. "Say nothing!" But there was no way for them to hear me. Nor did they seem to notice her lurking there outside the door. They had too much trust in me, it seemed.

"David, if there's a chance we can stop this, we need to stop it. We're wasting time debating it! People's lives are at stake. We can't just ignore that to save ourselves."

"And we can't just send our people to be slaughtered either."

"We wouldn't be! We have a name." Owen was starting to yell. The robot would probably have been able to overhear his half of the conversation even without the door cracked open.

"Owen, have you considered the possibility that they—" he hesitated, taking care with his words, "—changed Mackenzie?"

"What? No. She's just a little shell shocked."

"Maybe. But the fact that she doesn't remember what happened to her, but she does remember rather detailed information about the plot against Coda is too convenient for my taste. It feels like a trap."

"Yes!" I shouted to the voice. "They're not as stupid as you'd like to think." A very self-satisfied grin spread across my face as I folded my arms over my chest.

"You're absolutely right. It could be a trap." Owen sat back in his chair. "But if it's not, tens of thousands of people will die."

TWENTY-ONE

The projection became jerky, and I didn't hear any more of the conversation as the robot was grabbed and roughly thrown into one of the training rooms.

After a few blinks, Mitchell came into focus. Mitchell wasn't normally forward or aggressive like this. Something was up. I got up and moved closer to the screen, as if that would help me understand what he was thinking.

Whirling around, he shut the door behind him and backed the robot up against the nearest wall.

"Tell me something, Mackenzie." He placed emphasis on my name. "What makes a good sundae?"

I was practically nose to nose with the projection, willing her to defy him, to give him a wrong answer, anything. But all she did was stare at him, seemingly cowed into silence. But I knew better. The puppeteers didn't *know* the answer.

"I don't know what's going on yet," he said, his voice low and threatening. "But I'm going to get to the bottom of it. Everyone is blinded by their happiness to see you. But they've done something to you, and I can tell it ain't good." He was right in the robot's face, bracing himself with one hand on either side of her against the wall he had her backed up against. Under different circumstances, an outsider might think he was about to ravish her.

But the robot was remarkably unaffected by his threats. She didn't flinch when he got in her face, her breathing never quickened, and I was willing to bet her stone-faced expression had not changed.

"I'm watching you. And when I figure out what's going on, you better hide." He pounded the wall near her head, but she still didn't flinch. Then he left her alone in the room.

After a few moments, she calmly exited the training room and went upstairs to her own bedroom.

Mitchell knew. Of course he knew. He knew what it was like to be tortured by the Potestas, what it did to a person. But this was different, and he could tell. And thank God for that.

"What now?" I asked the projection, feeling hopeful Mitchell would figure it out any minute. Then we could fight this together. I wouldn't be alone.

"Tomorrow, your love will die," the voice said, very matter of fact.

"You don't know that. David might not even let him go."

"We shall see," the voice said, leaving an ominous feeling to the air that was hard to ignore.

The robot stared at the ceiling of my room. "Get up," I said to her. I needed to know what Owen was doing, and yet she refused to move. "Get up, you worthless piece of—"

A knock at her door silenced my swearing.

She got up and went to the door rather stiffly. David was on the other side. "Owen isn't here with you, is he?"

The robot blinked at him, and I saw David push past the robot and search my room. "Damn it," he whispered, more to himself than to the robot.

"Where is he?" I called to David. "Where is he?"

David sat on my keyboard's stool and leaned on his knees. "I told him it was too dangerous to go to the university on his own. I didn't make the decision lightly. He openly disagreed with me, but I remained adamant. It's become clear that he went anyway, and he apparently took a few people with him. I don't know if I should send someone after them, or if it would mean I'm just sending more sheep to the slaughter."

"Go after him! Bring him back before Coda can happen! I'll do it myself!" I called out to the projection.

"How gallant of you," the voice said. If it had a face, I knew it would've given me a mocking smile. "Unfortunately for you, you'll do no such thing. Look around you, Mackenzie. You do as I say. And I say you're going to watch your friends die. Every last one of them, starting with Owen."

"How am I supposed to watch Owen die if I'm not there? If he dies at Coda, there will be nothing left of his body. Zero will reduce him to ash, and you know it."

"A valid point. However, I'm willing to live with that small imperfection."

Well, I'm not, I thought to myself, knowing I had to find a way out before it was too late.

TWENTY-TWO

L ooking out across the beautiful mountain lake as I sat on the deck of my nightmare dream home, I came to a resolution. I would fight harder. There was nothing to lose by trying.

I took a deep breath as I sat in a chair I hoped never to see again. Closing my eyes, I emptied my mind of everything. All the grief, anger, guilt, and fear that had been my constant companions for months poured out of me until my mind had nothing inside it, nothing but the sound of my breathing. I didn't think about Owen, Tracy, or even Maddie. Only breathing. In. Out.

The quiet was rather calming for me, and I hated to abandon it so soon, but there was work to be done. So I stretched out my mind and searched for any sign of Shields. At first, it felt like an odd thing to do, like I was one of those Russian dolls or something—a mind lost within a mind, looking for a mind.

Lacking any tangible experience in this arena, I floundered at first, finding no sign of my captor. But I had nothing but time on my hands, so I kept at it. With my eyes closed, I continued to search the darkness. My paradise hell didn't exist behind the security of my eyelids. Here, there was only darkness, where there was nowhere and everywhere to hide.

The darkness was peaceful in a way I'd never understood before. While I was lost in grieving for Maddie, I'd allowed it to consume me completely. But this was so much more serene. The quiet wasn't lonely; it was welcome, offering me time to breathe.

I had no idea how long I searched the darkness with my mind. Without watching the projection, I had no way to keep track of the passage of time. It didn't matter. Not anymore. I operated in a sort of Schrodinger's Cat world. Owen existed, and at the same time, he didn't. I wouldn't know for sure until I freed myself from the box. So that remained my focus—open the box.

Eventually, I realized I was no longer alone in the darkness. I came across a small block. It looked like a child's wooden building block, with an uppercase letter T on one side and a picture of a toothbrush on the other. Examining it more closely, I noticed the top had a different image, and as I looked at it, the image started to move. It was Shields, standing at the mirror, brushing his teeth. He wore a towel around his waist and leaned close to the mirror to inspect his face as he brushed. His dark, curly hair dripped a little when he ran his free hand through it. And that was all. The memory played again, looking exactly the same as it had the first time.

I held the memory in my hand and looked at it. *Such a small building block*, I thought as I closed my hand around it and started to squeeze. At first, the corners of the block dug into my hand, but I kept right on squeezing. I could feel the memory starting to give under the pressure, and soon a fine, sawdust-like material started to seep through my fingers and form a small pile at my feet.

"Just what do you think you're doing?" a familiar voice asked me. I knew it was Shields, but he sounded different... almost desperate. The balance of power had shifted.

I ignored him I settled down beside the pile and blew, forever scattering the first of many memories I hoped to destroy. As I scattered the memory dust, the darkness seemed to press in around me, as if it was imploding on itself.

"I will kill you before you finish whatever it is you hope to accomplish," the voice threatened. If he killed me, it would be over—they would lose their weapon. If he didn't, I would kill him. Either way, I won.

Silently, I pressed on and found more and more building blocks to destroy. The blocks formed a nice little pile at my feet. Each time I picked one up, two or three new ones appeared in its place.

His memories were odd, unimportant, and scattered all over the timeline of his life, not linear like other memories I'd seen.

I got very excited about one memory in particular, thinking I'd found what I was looking for, but that feeling waned when I started to watch it.

It had a capital P on one side and a lightning bolt on another. *Power?* I wondered? *Potestas?*

The memory showed Shields in front of another man, but I couldn't hear what they were saying. It was too muffled, save for a few words I could make out through their mumbling. Things like "Unseen," "Coda," and "Dr. Jeppe." The image became so hazy, I could barely see the two figures through the fog, and I had no hope of understanding the things they were saying. Something important was in there, but it had been deliberately obscured from me.

Frustrated, I threw the memory to the ground and crushed it beneath my foot, ignoring the surrounding darkness as it closed in around me.

"Stop it!" the voice yelled, but it sounded more muted than it had before.

Whether Shields was scrambling his memories to protect himself, or the Potestas had programmed him to protect their own secrets, I wasn't sure. What I did know was that the method was effective. But if Shields' mind was built this way, how did he function? How did he remember anything at all?

I pondered their methods as I crushed memory after memory, the darkness closing in on me each time, the voice becoming little more than a whisper as its protests continued.

The task so consumed me, I barely even noticed. I was intent on stopping the Potestas, on preventing them from learning more about the Unseen. More than that, I had to eliminate the threat to Owen, Mitchell, and David—my family. I had to break free so I could find Owen, and then I could concentrate on the other threats. Destroying Shields from within was my best hope.

I couldn't help but wonder what was happening to his body as I wreaked havoc on his brain. Didn't the people around him notice something was happening? Maybe he was alone, with no one around to help him. Maybe he was beyond help. I could only hope that was the case.

Finally, I came to his last memory. The darkness was so close, pressing down in on me, making it hard to breathe. I'd stopped watching the memories ages ago, but I was curious about this last memory. So heavily guarded, buried deeply among all the others, it had to be something special. Peering into the block, I found myself in a hospital room. A woman with sweaty, long brown hair lay in the bed with a bundle in her arms. Tears streamed down her face as she gazed down at the sleeping baby. Machines beeped and nurses bustled around, but I barely noticed them. All I saw was the woman and the baby. Shields put one tender hand on the baby, and then leaned in to kiss the woman.

Pulling back in horror, I hesitated with the memory in my hands. This tiny, wooden block was probably all that kept me in the Potestas' prison. But the image of the baby stayed my hand. He had a family. The knowledge was hard to digest. Did they know his plans for the world? Were they also members of the Potestas? For their sake, I almost hoped they were. Otherwise, they'd be in a lot of danger.

The memory tumbled from my hand at the thought. Whose side was I on? Anger bubbled up inside me. I didn't want to have to take sides, but if I did, I always and inevitably would choose the side of life.

I reached over and picked the little, wooden block back up, which proved difficult in the tight space. The Unseen didn't plan to murder thousands and thousands of people. They were trying to save those lives. And so was I.

"I'm sorry," I whispered to the baby as I crushed the last memory in my hand, knowing he would never hear me, but hoping he would one day forgive me for killing his father.

As the darkness caved in around me, crushing me, I sent out a silent prayer. At first, I wasn't sure what I was praying for. My own soul? Owen's safety? Peace for Mitchell and David? The end of the Potestas? In the end, it was all of the above.

The weight on my spectral body was excruciating. My head felt like it was going to explode, right along with my chest and my arms and legs. I tried to push back, but there was nothing to push back against.

I cried out in fear and pain, and then it was over.

TWENTY-THREE

I sat up in bed, so drenched in sweat that the sheets were soaked. The room around me was blurry. Blinking a few times did nothing to bring it into focus.

Much to my dismay, no one was sitting at my bedside. The robot had hardly encouraged such attention, but I'd hoped Mitchell wouldn't leave her unattended. I would have to speak with him about that. And where had David gone? Regretting that I hadn't witnessed the rest of their conversation, I now had no idea if he'd sent others after Owen. For all I knew, days could have passed.

The room spun as I took my first real steps in weeks. I collapsed a few feet from the door and crawled the rest of the way.

Help. The word kept repeating over and over in my mind, a constant mantra that kept me moving.

Clawing my way to the door handle, I fumbled clumsily with the lock. Of course the robot had locked it. Why wouldn't she have? She wasn't one of the Unseen. She was a danger that had lurked among them.

Finally, the lock released and I tumbled out into the hall, dangling from the door handle. I scanned both directions wildly, not trusting what my eyes saw to be reality. Mitchell's words echoed in my mind: *They made it very difficult for me to differentiate*

between the world they'd created and reality. It left me angry sometimes.
They'd destroyed the person I was.

Had the Potestas destroyed the person I was? Then I remembered the things I'd done in my grief—the selfish way I'd pursued my own goals and aims. If they had annihilated my past self, was that such a bad thing?

Shaking my head, I tried to focus, but fear suddenly crippled me. What if I were somehow still in Shields' mind? Could this be one of the Potestas' games?

"Shields!" I cried out. "You coward! Talk to me!" As I crawled down the hall, my sweaty hand went out from under me and I smacked my face on the ground.

When there was no sign of the voice—no laughter or snide comments—hysteria bubbled up inside me. "Is this your idea of some kind of joke?" I asked, scanning the empty hall. Where was everyone? Was this just another corridor in Shields' mind? Was I still trapped inside him after all?

"Is this just a new prison you've created? Well, bravo." I rolled over onto my back, but I couldn't raise my arms to clap like I intended.

Mitchell's face materialized within my line of site. It was stricken with suspicion, tempered with the tiniest flash of concern. I frowned at him. "You're an asshole," I said to the voice.

"I'm not real fond of you right now either," Mitchell said as he lifted me into his arms, and then everything went dark.

When I woke up, there was a cool cloth on my head. Mitchell leaned against the far wall, while David sat on the edge of my bed.

Mitchell noticed me stirring first, but he just stared at me, saying nothing. I managed to get David's attention by bumping him with my leg. He was solid. Warm. Real. He turned toward me.

Sitting up too quickly, I threw myself into his arms. He held me as the worst head rush of my life passed over me. "This is real," I breathed into his chest.

David held me out at arm's length and searched my eyes.

"Of course this is real. What do you mean?"

I leaned back, but nothing was there to support me, and I ended up flouncing back onto the bed. "Where do I start?" I said in a small voice, managing to prop myself up on my elbows. It was all so confusing. Though I wanted to believe this was real—that I'd truly escaped—it was hard to trust that impulse.

"Mitchell," I whispered. He would be able to tell me if this was real.

David narrowed his eyes. "Mitchell has not exactly been your best advocate lately. I'm surprised you want to talk to him."

Hope brought a sliver of a smile to my face as my eyes went to Mitchell. He continued to glare at me. "Is that so?"

"He thinks you aren't to be trusted, that we shouldn't discuss sensitive matters in front of you. He even went so far as to suggest we expel you from our ranks." The conflict played out on my father's face plainly. I could tell he wasn't willing to expel the daughter he lost twice. But I could also tell he didn't fully trust me after whatever Mitchell had said to him—it was obvious from his tone of his voice and the way he'd pulled away from our embrace. It was hard to ignore the fact that he was not touching me in any way anymore.

"He's right. Or at least, he was." Both men gaped at me. "Please, Mitchell."

He approached the bed cautiously. "What do you want?"

"Mitchell, what makes a really good ice cream sundae?" I asked, not even trying to hide the desperation in my voice.

He moved closer to me, his suspicion bordering on hostility. "Why should I tell you?"

David interrupted. "You want to talk about ice cream?"

"I could tell you if you asked me," I begged, ignoring David. This moment had to be real. It just had to be.

He hesitated, either debating his options or my sincerity. And those mere seconds felt like absolute torture. If I were still in Shields' mind, he'd taken torture to a whole new level, practically erasing the lines between reality and the prison.

After an eternity, Mitchell finally spoke up. "Fine, then. What makes a really good ice cream sundae, Mac?" he asked as he folded his arms over his chest, confident I wouldn't answer.

"Homemade caramel."

His arms dropped and his face lit up. His approach was slow and deliberate, but I saw a flicker of hope in his eyes that hadn't been there before. I imagined the same emotion could be found in my own expression.

"Mac?" he asked as he reached out for me.

"Is this real?" I asked him, tears making it hard to see him, but I refused to blink them away. If I did, he might dissolve into the voice's laughter.

"It's real."

And still the voice didn't come, and neither did the projection screen. I searched wildly for it in the room, but I came up empty.

"What are you looking for?" David asked.

"The screen. The projection that showed me you."

"What?" David asked, but Mitchell got quiet, his face turning sad.

"You were in there all along." Mitchell said it like a statement, not a question.

"Yes." We sat in knowing silence for a few moments, but then David apparently couldn't take it anymore.

"Would either of you care to enlighten me on what the hell is going on here?"

After propping a few pillows against the wall behind the bed, I managed to sit all the way up and get myself comfortable. I knew it was going to be a long explanation. Just before I began, a thought occurred to me.

"Where is Owen?"

Their expressions turned sad.

"He's in the hospital."

Panic and hope battled for space in my exhausted mind. He was alive, but not well enough to be with me. "How long was I out? I was hoping I'd free myself in time to go to campus and save him."

"Coda happened two days ago. You have been locked in your room since our last meeting," David said with confusion in his voice..

"Just tell me what happened."

"We didn't manage to put a stop to Coda. My contact at Homeland Security refused to cancel the event, or even move it to a more secure location, without more evidence. Their initial investigation of Professor Peterson turned up nothing—rightfully so, as it turns out—so they filed it as a false lead." The scowl on his face did little to hide his frustration.

I tried not to think about his words. *Unsuccessful.* How many lives had been lost?

"As I understand it, the musicians were never told of the danger. The event went on as planned. Over a thousand people were killed."

Shock and horror washed over me, but then another thought registered. "Wait, only a thousand?" I asked. The Potestas had hoped for a much larger number of casualties.

"It was still a lot of people." I thought I heard a hint of frustration in David's voice. "But Owen and a few other rogue members of our group were able to save most of the people who were there. I still don't have all the details."

My heart filled with pride for the man I loved—and also broke for those he hadn't managed to save.

Looking to Mitchell, I asked, "A few others?"

Mitchell nodded. "I was there. But I got out."

I nodded, knowing what that meant to him—that he'd gotten out while his best friend was hanging on to life by a thread. He wouldn't see himself as a hero, only the one who'd escaped unscathed.

"Unfortunately, ISIS is being blamed," David continued. "They are denying involvement, but their word doesn't go very far. This could lead to war, Mackenzie, and that may be exactly what the Potestas are hoping for. I'm not sure what their ultimate goal is yet."

The words *the ultimate position of power* played in my head, but before I could get them out, David went on.

"The world is reeling, as you can imagine. I'm sure I don't have to tell you how devastated the music industry is by the loss. Many of the world's top musicians were lost in the attack. There have been dozens of memorials over the last few days, with more to come, I'm sure."

I slumped at that information. Some of the world's best musicians had lost their lives, and for what? Tears flowed silently down my cheeks, and I buried my face in my hands as David rested a hand on my leg.

"Would you like to see Owen?"

My head snapped up. There was nothing I wanted more in the whole world than to see him. Touch him. Kiss him.

"Take me to him, now."

Mitchell helped me out of bed, and we walked over to the stairwell. But instead of going up, toward the garage, we went down.

"Where are we going?"

"To see Owen," David said simply, as if the answer should be obvious.

"But, isn't he in the hospital?"

"He's in our hospital, on site."

I should've known. Of course we had our own hospital. Too many wounded in public hospitals would raise questions, not to mention it would leave our patients vulnerable and exposed.

Many of the Unseen we passed stared at me with open distrust in their eyes.

There are many partially burned bridges to repair, I see. The robot did well.

David continued with his explanation as we walked.

"Owen…" He trailed off, and I held on to Mitchell desperately, both because I wasn't sure I could handle hearing about Owen's injuries and because I needed help navigating the stairs. "Owen is lucky to be alive. Quite frankly, I have no idea how he managed it. We haven't gotten his side of the story yet. He's been unconscious since he was found."

"Found?" I asked. How had he not been reduced to ash by the chemical if he'd still been at Coda when it was released?

"I have my own theories about what happened," David explained. Mitchell looked down the staircase, listening but not commenting, as was his way.

"Let's hear it." My voice broke, betraying me.

"I believe Owen tried to talk to Professor Peterson and remove her from the school, but he was mistaken about her being a threat. I can only assume the... robot... provided her name because she was on your mind. As you know, she was a complete dead end. After that, he and the other Unseen who were with him managed to stop the performances on two of the three stages. They evacuated that part of the campus rather effectively by pulling fire alarms and calling in bomb threats—old school, but effective in a pinch. Owen somehow ended up being locked in a secure location by campus security. I don't know if he was caught pulling an alarm or what. But I believe they were waiting for the police to come get him when the festival was slated to start. Because of his proximity to the site, he had minimal exposure to Zero. Those in his building have had a forty percent survival rate so far. He's included in that statistic."

Forty percent. It echoed in my mind. *I came so close to losing him.*

"Will he wake up?" I asked, not sure I wanted to hear the answer.

"Most likely, yes. He's in a chemical coma now, while his body heals from the damage." David paused as he navigated the stairwell.

"Damage?" I asked, picturing him permanently confined to a hospital bed, nothing more than a vegetable for the rest of his life, all because I hadn't gotten out in time.

"Third-degree burns cover about twenty percent of his body. His neck, left shoulder, and both hands all the way up his arms were severely affected by the chemical. We assume his arms took the brunt of the outer damage because he used them to shield himself. But he also incurred a fair amount of damage to his lungs. The hospital is working hard to repair it, but considering how they've never dealt with this chemical before, they're having a hard time knowing what to do. It's a trial-and-error process at this point."

"Will he be functional?"

"Yes," Mitchell answered firmly without looking at me.

David tried to catch his eye, but Mitchell continued to focus on the stairs.

"The doctors believe he will. He may not run any marathons, but I don't think he was too fond of running in the first place," David filled in. "Unless it involved chasing after you."

A small smile formed on my face in response to David's remark, but it didn't feel real. None of it did. "How long will he be...?" I trailed off, not really sure how to complete the sentence.

"Until it's time," David answered vaguely. "Are you ready to see him?"

"More than," I said as we stood at the very bottom of the stairwell.

David touched a seemingly inane panel on the wall. The outline of his hand illuminated, and the floor beneath us slowly lowered, catching me by surprise. Mitchell took my elbow for support, and we went deeper into the depths of the facility.

At the bottom, a sterile room awaited us. It looked remarkably similar to a real hospital. White walls and horrible florescent lights surrounded us, but there weren't as many beds, and not nearly as many nurses or doctors bustling around. There was no receptionist to receive us, probably because it was assumed we knew where we were going. The technology that lined the walls was astounding. Some screens showed x-rays of various body parts; others showed vital statistics.

"Are those all for Owen?"

"No, he was the most badly hurt, but he's not the only one down here. Camden will be ready to go back upstairs today, I expect."

Camden too? The thought threatened to break my heart even more.

We finally arrived at Owen's room. Though I'd thought I was ready, nothing could've prepared me for seeing him that way. He was connected to a dozen tubes and wires. A machine hissed rhythmically as it breathed for him. His neck and arms were covered in white bandages that already had stains seeping through them, but his face looked as I remembered it.

Mitchell led me over to Owen's good side and sat me in a chair. I stroked Owen's face and started talking, not sure if he could hear me, but knowing what I needed to say.

"Owen, my love, I'm so sorry." Leaning forward, I stroked his face, feeling how warm it was. How real.

"We can leave you two alone if you like," David offered, shifting awkwardly.

"No. Now that we're all together, I'd like to tell you what happened." I paused, trying to take strength from the love that surrounded me. These men were all so important to me. Silently, I vowed to never take them for granted again.

"I don't really know where to start. Going in to get Shields seemed like a good plan, but something went terribly wrong." My own voice sounded distant to me as I struggled to find words to explain how horribly I'd failed. "It started with Tracy. He got her easily, too easily. Then he trapped me inside my own personal hell." I couldn't bring myself to look at Mitchell. I had no idea what they'd done to Mitchell, nor did I want to know. My own personal paradise/hell had been quite enough.

"I watched on some kind of projection screen from the inside of Shields' mind as Amanda, of all people, explained what they were planning—how they would use me to infiltrate the Unseen's facility. They had control of my body, although they didn't use that control as well as they should have."

I continued stroking Owen's undamaged face, holding on to this reality with everything I had. It might be broken, but it was real.

"No. I took to thinking of her as a robot. Her movements were so stiff, I had to laugh as I watched her climb the stairs. I thought they'd get me killed just trying to maneuver my body. But, unfortunately, they didn't. She made it all the way down to your office, David, and I'm afraid of what they've learned."

David sank into a chair behind me. "I um…" He trailed off, a stunned expression on his face. He spoke through his hand over his mouth. "I had hoped I was wrong about Amanda."

After a long pause, I swallowed and told them the rest.

"There's more. Coda was just a test run, or maybe even a diversion. I don't really know. In any case, the Potestas intend to use Zero for more attacks. Something about getting into a position of power."

"How can we stop them?" Mitchell asked, a hint of fear in his voice. He'd lived through the Coda disaster. He had probably been out there helping Owen. Being trapped in Shields' mind had at least saved me from seeing the devastation of that day firsthand. And yet, the memory of those screaming monkeys came back to me full force, and seeing the evidence of that horrible chemical all over my love's broken body brought tears to my eyes The knowledge of the damage that had been done to so very many people made them flow freely down my cheeks.

We couldn't allow it to happen ever again, let alone on a wider scale. But I had no idea where to begin. I looked to David for answers. Mitchell was staring at him too, I noticed.

"Mackenzie, as soon as you are feeling a little better, we will have a detailed debrief," David said. "You will tell me everything you know, and I mean every last detail. Something you've witnessed will help us." Although it was a statement, it came out sounding a bit like a prayer.

"There's one more thing." Taking a deep breath, I dove in. "I'm sorry. I wanted to say that to all of you." I looked at the men, each with a different expression on his face. Mitchell seemed understanding, David seemed caught off guard, and Owen...

"I know who the real enemy is now, not to mention the devastation they're capable of wreaking. I know it's not about me, or my grief, or the fact that my family was torn apart by these maniacs. More families will be torn apart by them if they're not stopped." I thought of Shields' family, and how I'd just torn them apart, and sighed. "I understand sacrifices will need to be made for the greater good, but I also know my personal vendetta has gotten in my way. It has hindered my ability to serve the Unseen."

Looking down at Owen's face, I stroked his forehead with my thumb. His eyes were closed, but he looked anything but peaceful with the huge tube coming unnaturally out of his mouth, held in place by tape on both sides.

"The Potestas have a lot of interesting techniques I don't believe they're using to their full potential. I'd like to learn more, and perhaps we can perfect their techniques for use against them. Tracy would've wanted that." I swallowed a hitch in my throat.

Sighing, I let all the questions, doubts, grief, and anger whoosh out of me with one long breath.

"I promise, from now on, I will be undivided."

TWENTY-FOUR

I wanted to stay by Owen's side until he woke up, but the nurse shooed me out, saying I needed to eat, sleep, and "for God's sake, shower." It gave me a little comfort to think about all the ways I'd be there for him when he woke up—just like he'd been there for me.

Sleep evaded me, but the piano finally summoned me. I found my way to the baby grand for the first time in weeks. Gaspard flowed from my fingers better than ever, as if I'd never taken a break. Yes, I missed a note here and there, but it felt wonderful to be lost in the music again. I wasn't the same person I'd been the last time I played, but I'd *survived*. And I'd come out stronger for it.

David and Mitchell, apparently night owls themselves, stopped by once or twice and listened for a bit, but I didn't stop. I needed the music.

When my fingers finally started to ache, I reluctantly quit, but the music stayed with me.

A woman's voice interrupted my peace. "That was lovely." Her voice was calm and soothing, despite the fact I hadn't known she was there. Based on the sound, I knew she was in the back corner of the library.

I stretched over the top of the piano and spotted her sitting under a soft lamp with some sort of knitting and a ball of yarn. She had long, brown hair and beautiful, chocolate-colored eyes.

"Have we met?" I asked, not sure if the robot had met her, or if she was totally new.

"No. I'm Rebecca. I will be taking over training at this facility." There was no arrogance in her tone, but her statement made me bristle a little. I didn't want to train with anyone else.

Sensing my discomfort, she set her project down and walked over. "I knew Tracy well. We trained together as new recruits." Leaning against the piano, she looked into my eyes with kindness. "I'm deeply saddened by the circumstances that brought me here. But I would be lying if I said I wasn't excited by the opportunity to work with you." I couldn't help but return her smile.

Holding out my hand for her to shake, I said, "It's nice to meet you, Rebecca. I'm Mackenzie, Mac for short."

"Let's hear a little more, hm? I'm not quite ready for bed," she asked.

So, I cracked my aching fingers and dove in to another round of Gaspard, this time slowing it down, taking care with the notes, measures, and melodies, letting the music fill the room completely.

We had a lot of work ahead of us, and even more lives would be at stake, but in that moment, I knew down deep that we would prevail. I knew it like I knew how to breathe.

After all, I was not alone at the piano, and I no longer felt unforgiven.

Did you enjoy this book?
Let the author know!
Leave a review!

ACKNOWLEDGMENTS

First, thanks be to God, for His glorious gifts to my family and me. I've been afforded the time to write, the money to fund the books, and the ability to craft stories and characters I love. For these things, and so much more, I am grateful.

Second, thank you so much to my wonderful husband. You are the logic to my emotion, the rock to my ocean, and I can't wait to see how far we can go together.

To my team, what can I say? You guys are freaking amazing. Jamie, my constant beta, even when she's off to Europe in like two days, makes time to read my crap. Where would I be without you? Angela and Cynthia, my editors, your turd polish is something I need to get the recipe for. Because when I hand you a steaming pile of you-know-what, I get back solid gold and I love it! Thank you! And of course, the amazing designers at Damonza, your covers continue to be works of art. Hats off to you!

My friends, Mary and Dannie, I love you. You curse at my failures and toast my victories, even if I just have pop in my glass. I couldn't ask for better friends.

And of course, Christian. You've helped me so much with this career change. Despite the fact that you're technically my boss, you're one of my biggest cheerleaders, and will spend hours talking book covers and word count with me. I hope you know how much you are loved and appreciated.

My family, I love you (the mostest). And Shane, you're a pain but I'll make a reader out of you yet. Seriously, thank you for reading my stuff, and for your genuine support.

This time, I have a few special thanks as well. Shannon Mayer, I am so lucky to count you among my colleagues, and more importantly, my friends. Thank you for your continued council and help. I'm forever in your debt.

And The Literary Connoisseur. Words cannot express how much I heart you. Friends, if you're looking for an awesome book blog, hers is it. Your passion for the written word is astounding. Thank you so much for your support.

Lastly, thank *you*, dear reader. You've sacrificed most of all for this book, your time. For that, I am deeply grateful.

I'll see you in September.

—S

ABOUT THE AUTHOR

Stephanie Erickson is an English Literature graduate from Flagler College. She lives in Florida with her family. Unforgiven is her fifth novel.

Stephanie loves to connect with readers! Follow her on Facebook at http://www.facebook.com/stephmerickson, Twitter @sm_erickson.

Check out her Web site at www.stephanieericksonbooks.com where you can catch up on the latest news and coming events. Be sure to sign up for the newsletter while you're there, and you'll be the first to hear about new releases, upcoming promotions and more!